Praise for
They Could Live with Themselves

In the final story of Jodi Paloni's *They Could Live with Themselves*, a young man who aspires to be a photographer decides "to do a series, tell a story" in "twelve images" and "invite his audience to feel." That's what Paloni does in this masterly collection of linked stories set in fictional Stark Run, Vermont, where she introduces us to an astonishingly wide range of characters and makes us feel deeply about them and their desires, their fears, their joys, and their sorrows. The town and its people come so utterly to life that no matter where you're from you'll feel like you're home. Stark Run may not appear on any of Rand McNally's maps, but it's an important addition to America's literary map, one that ranks up there with the likes of Sherwood Anderson's Winesburg, OH, and Elizabeth Strout's Crosby, Maine. I suggest that you visit Stark Run, and soon. If you do, you may leave it, but it and its characters will never leave you.

— David Jauss, author of *Glossolalia: New & Selected Stories*

Reading Jodi Paloni's *They Could Live with Themselves* is akin to sitting down at a small-town bar or diner in Vermont and eavesdropping on people's stories. You'll immediately feel the startling intimacies between characters, and each tale progressively unspools the charms, troubles, and triumphs of the small community, even as some ache to leave it all behind. A stirring portrait of rural New England, complete with lush, almost ethereal descriptions of the landscapes, this is a collection that you will savor long after the last page.

— Matthew Limpede, Executive Editor, *Carve Magazine*

Throughout these wise stories, Jodi Paloni demonstrates the human ability to continue on in the face of the unexpected, or more often, the expected, the inevitable, the routine. Her prose reflects her Vermont setting: sparse, restrained, with bursts of beauty and emotional resonance. Her characters—teachers and students, business owners and artists—surprise themselves (and us) with realizations that, quite often, arrive late, but never—Paloni assures us—too late. She writes with compassion and subtlety, reminding us of the ways that we are all connected and the ways that we must each, alone, learn to live with ourselves.

– Lori Ostlund, author of *The Bigness of the World*, winner of the Flannery O'Connor Award for Short Fiction

They Could Live with Themselves

To: Elizabeth → Enjoy reading, and thanks so much for your support! 3/16 ♡

They Could Live
with Themselves

Linked Stories

Jodi Paloni ♡

Jodi Paloni

Press 53
Winston-Salem

Press 53, LLC
PO Box 30314
Winston-Salem, NC 27130

First Edition

Cover design and layout by Kevin Morgan Watson

Cover art, "Red Fence" Copyright © 2012
by Dawn D. Surratt, used by permission of the artist.
instagram.com/ddhanna

Author photo by Lisa McCoy

Printed on acid-free paper
ISBN 978-1-941209-38-7

For Bob, Best Beloved

and

In Memory of Christy Bailey

Acknowledgments

The author wishes to thank the editors and staff of the publications where the following stories first appeared.

"Molly Sings the Blues," *Whitefish Review, Lucky #13*, June 2013

"Deep End," *Short Story America Volume IV Anthology*, September 2015, Winner of the Short Story America Prize

"The Third Element," *Carve Magazine*, Fall, 2012, Second Place in the 2012 Raymond Carver Short Story Contest

"From Inside," *Green Mountains Review*, October 2013

"Accommodations," *upstreet*, Issue 8, Summer 2012

"The Air of Joy," *Connotation Press*, May 2015

Contents

Molly Sings the Blues

M olly cherishes an empty house and no one around for miles. She cranks up a scratchy Billie Holiday album on the old turntable in the den. In the kitchen, she grabs her broom, gripping the wooden handle like a microphone in the same way she clutched her hairbrush as a girl when she pretended to be Cher in front of the bathroom mirror.

She slides into the living room, takes pleasure in sounds that slip around her body—saxophone, piano, a brush stroking a drum, and the heady croon of Billie. They're all here, these sounds, all here to help Molly lose herself or become more of who she wanted to be or perhaps a little of both. She imagines her skin dark and silky, and the space around her a smoky nightclub. She leans in towards the broom, then away, mimicking the lilting rhythms. The word she thinks of: languid. The picture of herself: inches taller and pounds thinner.

Trilling the shimmering melodies, she slithers a hand up and down her hip and sashays across the pinewood floors. She lifts her chin. Her eyelids close. Is it too late to learn how to sing, she wonders, to really sing, deep and throaty like Billie, the blues, to buy a piano, take lessons, make some strides to catch-up, this one life, to draw herself from the well, draw the wilderness out of the woman within the wife, the mother? Is it too late to exchange one kind of life for something altogether new?

Most days, she plays the album, tucks her broom away, and then sits at the farm table to enjoy leftovers topped with ketchup on a crusty roll, a smidge more solitude before her tall bright son, the youngest, breezes in from the career center. But today, as the last song winds down, a shadow movement in the front yard beckons her to the picture window. A young woman sits on the wooden swing hanging from the maple tree by the barn. She's brushing her hair. Molly squints in the sun, searching for an unfamiliar car in the driveway. There is none. Though the stranger looks harmless, harm has been done; the woman has seen her. Molly now feels as if there are bugs crawling on the inside of her clothes.

A rush of red-winged blackbirds swoops and scatters. The woman stands. She's pregnant, bloated low on a thin frame. She wears pink leggings and a white t-shirt stretched and baggy below her knees. Molly wonders how far she walked in leather fashion boots when the woman flicks her wrist in a low wave, then stretches both arms above her head, and arches her back. She slings an over-sized handbag over her shoulder and approaches the kitchen porch.

Up close, Molly recognizes her. Crystal Townsend. She was fifteen the summer Jack hired her to help Molly on the family beach vacation in Maine, though Molly had told Jack she could look after her own kids. An experiment, Jack said, to give Molly a chance to breathe.

Some years ago, Molly heard that Crystal ended up in a women's detention center for writing bad checks. There may have been a drug habit. It doesn't matter. What matters is how long the woman's been gawking through the window and why the hell she's here. Molly greets Crystal at the screen door; what else can she do?

Crystal pets the rosemary in a hanging pot, spilling dirt onto Molly's clean porch. "I love that smell. I worked at a greenhouse once." The girl talks as if the two of them were in the middle of a conversation. "You don't remember me, do you?"

Molly tightens the grip on her broom handle. "Sure, I do. You haven't changed so much." And, in fact, she hasn't, thinks Molly. Although the woman would be about thirty-three by now, she looks like a young twenty-something.

Crystal laughs. "Well, I'm not exactly the same.

They both look down at the belly pressing up against the screen between them. Molly flushes. "True." She smiles, and then frowns.

She remembers what Crystal looked like the summer of 1994, her body long and soft, her greasy potato-brown hair, and how pale flesh squished over the rim of the girl's pink string bikini like baby fat. In fact, Crystal acted like a baby—some fuss about a dead crab—and Molly had another kid to watch, her four little ones *and* the babysitter, until Jack put Crystal on a bus back to Vermont.

"It's been eighteen years almost exactly," Crystal says. "Sky's eighteen."

Molly bristles, but nods. She knows how old her son is. But Sky was born after that summer vacation, so how does Crystal know Sky?

"Is Sky around?" Crystal asks. "He promised to drive me to my birthing class up in Springfield."

"Sky said that?" Molly steadies herself with her broom. She doesn't care for someone telling her something about one of her kids that she doesn't already know. "I know what you're thinking." Crystal shifts her handbag to her other shoulder. "Don't worry. The baby isn't his."

Molly hadn't thought that, is confused, and now feels relief. She musters some manners. "You can wait for Sky inside."

◆　　◆　　◆

In the house, Molly wonders if she should say something about the dancing, then tells herself it's best to pretend it didn't happen. Who cares what Crystal Townsend thinks? People do silly things every day. She returns the broom to the pantry and stands behind the counter of her kitchen island, places her palms on the cool soapstone, moored by the familiar.

"Sit down." Molly gestures to the kitchen table. "Do you want something to eat?"

"Sure. I'm starving." Crystal circles her belly in small jerky motions, but stands fixed near the porch door.

Static from the speakers playing the end of the spinning record scratches the strained atmosphere. "I'll just turn that off and be right back," says Molly.

Alone in the den, she puts the record back in its sleeve, then looks up at the ceiling and stretches her tongue out as far as it will go, releasing the tension in her neck, a trick she learned from a yoga workshop she took last month with Wren, her best buddy since high school. Molly looks through the window to the back pasture. Jeb, their old draft horse, paws the ground grubbing for something green. Betty's tail switches at black flies. She tells herself to pause, to notice the moment. Sunlight runs pink across post-winter grass as if to soothe afternoon into evening. This is the kind of slowing down that Molly craves. Sky will be here soon to deal with Crystal, then Jack will appear, then supper, then the time when she can stretch out under the print quilt in the guest room where she goes to bed at night. She fills her lungs with a restorative breath.

When Molly steps back into the kitchen, she finds Crystal standing in front of the open fridge, pinching raw vegetables right out of the roasting pan. Molly's eyebrows fly up. Lord knows what kind of dirt and germs are now crawling around the pork loin she prepared earlier for her family's dinner.

"Sorry," Crystal mumbles, chewing. She shuts the refrigerator door, licks her fingers, and walks around the large open kitchen, picking up framed photos from a shelf with oily fingers and setting them down in the wrong places.

"Have a seat," Molly says in a firm tone. Jack calls it her manners-and-homework voice. "I'll fix you some food." She sets out a loaf of warm bread and cheese, crosses her arms, and frowns while Crystal eats.

Molly glances at the clock. "How *do* you and Sky know each other?" she asks. "I thought you'd been away."

"From the career center. I do the books." Crystal sniffs between bites. "I studied accounting in prison." She looks Molly directly in the eye as if challenging her to cast judgment, but Molly's raised five teenagers; she knows how to maintain a neutral face.

"Sky's a cutie pie," Crystal says. "We have lunch sometimes. Good kid, but kind of a loner."

Kind of a loner. What could Crystal possibly know about it?

"Sky's always been quiet. He likes to get his work done." Molly knows it sounds lame, like talk at a parent/teacher conference. She hasn't been paying attention to Sky in the same way she did with the other kids when they were in high school. She feels tired most of the time, as if she's nestled in a soft sticky cocoon, waiting for the next stage of her life while other lives go on around her. Her solitude with Billie Holiday is the one time of day when she feels a stirring. It's when she glimpses possibility through a cracked door, a sliver of light shining in, and on the other side of the door, a mysterious gloaming.

Crystal reaches into her handbag and pulls out a liter bottle of diet coke, uncaps it, and takes a long drink.

Molly cringes. "Would you like some water, or maybe a glass of milk?" She watches Crystal's throat as she gulps down the soda like a turkey working on a grub. Molly raises her voice, as if Crystal has a hearing problem. "Milk. From Sky's heifer."

Crystal sets the bottle down on the table. White foam rises to the top. "Yes, I know what milk is, but I'm fine. I don't like the stuff right from the cow." She reaches into her bag and pulls out a beat-up blue ukulele, plucks a string or two, and begins to play. "You don't mind if I practice, do you?"

"Go right ahead." Molly waves a hand as if flicking a fly.

Crystal strums the out-of-tune instrument and sings in different keys, assaulting Molly's sensibilities while she does the dishes. Molly doesn't know what more she could possible say to this woman. She is grateful when Sky's old truck pulls up to the back of the house. The door creaks as he slams it shut.

Crystal stops strumming and stands. She rolls her shoulders. Molly tries not to stare at the dirty shirt stretched to display Crystal's swollen belly button.

Sky walks in through the mudroom. "Hey, Mom." To Molly, he sounds surprised that she, his mother, is standing in her own kitchen instead of a grungy pregnant woman. He glances at Crystal. "Hey."

"Crystal's been waiting for you." Molly wipes her hands on a dishtowel.

"I see that. You guys met." His head swings back and forth, looking at Crystal then Molly then Crystal. He's breathless and gleaming. Molly usually loves the fresh feel of the house when Sky gets home from school. Now he just seems worked-up.

"I thought we were meeting at the center," he says.

Crystal steps between Sky and Molly and cuffs him on the arm. "Sorry. I didn't go in today. Cramping." She fingers the base of her belly. "Does it still work for you to drive me?" She turns to Molly. "I'll pay for gas."

"No, you won't," Sky says. "I said I'd take you." Sky looks at his watch. "Mom, does it work for you?"

Molly is surprised to be included. She wonders how she is supposed to answer a question like that. No, you're not allowed because . . . Because why? Because your father wants you down at the hardware store; because you're only eighteen and this is not your problem; because the whole world gets crazier by the minute and you will absolutely not become part of any of it. Most days, Molly is eager for Sky's launch into an independent life. Today, she feels left standing on the edge of a precipice.

"Check with your father. He wanted you to go with him to the meeting about the rummage sale." Her lips tighten. "Dinner's at seven." She hopes that doesn't sound like Crystal's invited.

Molly watches from the kitchen window as her son carries Crystal's scruffy bag and ridiculous ukulele to his truck. She sees them climb inside the cab. Crystal laughs at some grand gesture Sky makes with his hands. Are they making fun of Molly? Sky reverses the pickup in the driveway, spinning gravel as he turns the truck around. Molly continues to watch the back of the old Ford until there's only dust in the road. She clears the table, smelling the inside of the half-empty soda bottle. It's sugary like summer. She pours the thin liquid down the drain, listening to little bubbles hiss on the stainless steel and then watches them pop and disappear. The years of mothering have been like that, Molly thinks, fizzy, and then gone.

At the dinner table, Molly complains to Jack about Crystal.

"Sky's eighteen," Jack said. "Plus, you know how he is. He's always brought in strays. Remember that baby raccoon he fed all night? And that slew of kittens from the ditch he carried around in his backpack. He couldn't settle until they each had a home, and a good life, too, not just a corner in someone's barn."

"This is bad timing. Sky's still deliberating his acceptance letters. He's only got about five days unless he wants to stay stuck here going to community college like we did. He doesn't need this kind of distraction." She doesn't need a distraction either, Molly thinks. She's too close to the freedom that will come with Sky's independence. She worried about him all afternoon, his ability to make smart choices, his homework, car pile-ups, sexually transmitted diseases; you name it. When she adds up five kids and twenty-eight years of motherhood, it isn't the cooking and laundry, the sickness and homework, or the shuttling of bouncing youth around the universe that wore Molly out, it was the worry.

"What's wrong with community college?" Jack asks.

Molly glares.

"You're just riled up. Sky's just helping a friend," Jack says. "She's harmless."

"Harmless," Molly echoes.

He bends to kiss Molly on the cheek on his way out to the meeting. She sits like stone. The dirty dishes are piled on the table, all except for Sky's place setting, which remains untouched.

Sky drives in well after supper. From the living room, peering out at the lit-up barn from behind the dark of the curtains, Molly watches Sky move about, finishing up his chores. When he comes into the house, he doesn't look for her. He heads straight to his room.

Later, when Molly can't sleep, she prowls the house shrouded in new moon darkness. Jack won't notice that she's up. She's been sleeping in Trish's old room, now the guest room, for the past year, having blamed the move on hot flashes, saying she wakes up in the night and wants to read. What she really does in there is spread into a giant X in the middle of the bed. She listens to her breath in the dark. She wonders what's left for her and Jack and this life without kids at home. She wonders what else might be out there, something just for her.

Tonight she can't think at all. She shuts herself in the den, paces, and then takes a photo album from a shelf to the overstuffed couch. The cushions surrounding her smell of the barn from Jack's clothes. This comforts her. Flipping through pages, she finds the pictures she wants. The masking tape label at the top of the page reads, *Old Orchard Beach, August 1994,* the summer they fled their mountain farm and drove to Maine to spend a week at the shore.

She sees a photo of Trish wearing a one-piece suit, her body like a bone-thin boy. Trish is holding hands with Crystal in the surf. There's another one where the girls have fallen together, weak from laughter, sea foam pooling around their sprawled legs.

On the next page, three pictures: Baby Sarah asleep in her car seat beneath the umbrella, the twins digging for sand crabs, Jack snoozing in his chair. Molly remembers how Jack stirred and joined her near the surf. "The kids are having a good time, Moll. This was a good idea."

Molly looked up from the watery hole where she dug, but said nothing. Her husband's eyes dipped to her small breasts, flaccid in their black tankini top, the skin sucked dry from over a decade of nursing. She first felt pleased, and then repulsed that Jack's gaze fell into the top of her suit, disparate sensations sparring, somebody always needing something.

All of this comes back to Molly on the couch in the den, not as photographs, in still shots, but as if someone replays a film clip of the scene. She remembers how she dug in the sand even after the boys ran off to chase gulls, how she relished the rhythm of the senseless task, not knowing how to just sit in a beach chair all day.

Jack squatted next to her and rubbed the back of his knuckles across her shoulder. "You're getting a little red here."

"I'm fine." Molly straightened, waving off Jack's touch with the yellow shovel. She glanced towards the umbrella and the baby. Trish and Crystal strayed down the shoreline.

She was about to call the two girls when Crystal raced back to Molly and Jack, shrieked, and waved a large crab by one of its crooked pinchers. She wiggled it in Jack's face, laughing and teasing, her flesh wobbling as she flailed. Through her wet suit, Crystal's nipples pushed out against the skimpy triangles of fluorescent fabric. The swatch of bikini bottom revealed the texture of black wiry hair. Her arms and legs were covered in gooseflesh. Molly watched Jack notice the girl, too, how his eyes lingered on the triangles of the girl's bikini. She watched his expression tighten with surprise and then shame when he realized that Molly saw him gawking. Molly couldn't help it; she gave him her smug look as if to ask, what did I tell you? Jack grabbed Crystal's wrist and twisted it to keep the crab from touching his face.

"Put the crab back in the goddamn water, Crystal," Jack said, his voice crisp, struggling for control.

Crystal's eyes widened. She dropped the crab to the sand. It was dead.

The kids surrounded the crab. Jack let go of Crystal's wrist and returned to his chair where he sat staring at the sea. Molly studied her husband. He finally figured out that the girl was a mistake.

Crystal wailed that she wanted her mother. She jogged in place, shaking her hands, repeating over and over, "I just want to go home!"

"You'll be fine, Crystal. He barely touched you," said Molly. Then she softened. "Don't mind his yelling."

A lifeguard intervened, and Crystal wiped her snotty nose on the sun-kissed skin of her forearm and began to flirt. Jack walked with the baby to the water. The twins flicked sand over the limp crab, taking turns with the shovel. Trish gawked, shivering in her beach towel. Molly watched as if it were all happening in front of someone else's blanket and cooler. Later that afternoon, Jack put Crystal on a bus for home.

Now, in the den, Molly turns a page in the album: Jack with a new kite, Trish and the twins flying it, Sarah chewing on the yellow shovel on the blanket. Molly runs her fingers over the photographs, the ones of her family—just her family—the whole beach to themselves.

Some days Molly drives to town and can't remember all the reasons she went when she gets there, but these summer memories are precisely wedged in her mind. She wonders if Crystal arrived in her yard today, not to sabotage Sky's future, but to teach Molly something, to remind her that the scaffolding of a family is stacked precariously. Without strict vigilance, climbing into bed with the same husband night after night, crafting sensible applicable dreams, paying attention to who one allows in, the whole goddamn thing could crumble beyond repair.

It's past midnight now. She feels her mind claw for details; there was something else about that vacation. She studies the photos. She compares Crystal then, burgeoning with sexuality, to Crystal today, exuding hormones. How would Sky possibly avoid the woman's effect? Even Molly had succumbed, inadvertently, back then, to Crystal's prowess. Now Molly remembers the night in the motel after Jack sent Crystal home. Molly whispered to him in the dark. "Did you see the way that girl acted? I don't want her around Trish anymore. From now on, I'll take care of my own kids."

"I was trying to give you a goddamn break." Jack rolled onto his side, his back to Molly.

"You sure picked a winner."

Lying under the clammy sheets in the motel room, Molly thought about the way the girl's flesh had strained against her suit and how Crystal had expressed her needs and feelings freely. Molly used to be comfortable in her body before those four babies. She wanted her confidence back and she knew one sure way to get it. She slipped one of her legs, strong from horses and barn work, over Jack's hip, urging him easily to his back.

He rubbed his neck and scowled. "What now, Moll?"

Molly raised her nightgown above her hips and climbed to straddle him, something she had not done since Trish, their first born. She pressed her palms on his shoulders and closed her eyes against his disbelief. She slid against Jack until he pushed in. She thought of the babysitter's sheer lust for life, her total lack of propriety. She remembered her own teenage body and her first time with Jack. It had been a long time since they'd had sex. Months? Maybe even a year? Yes. It was over a year. She had been pregnant with Sarah.

She moved with Jack. She felt him meet her pace, slow and building to a fury that didn't last long. That night and the next and the next, kids dead to the world, Molly rolled towards Jack. He teased her about it for months, called it her awakening.

Of course, there were no photos of Molly and Jack under sandy motel sheets, but she remembers. One of those nights, Sky was conceived. In some strange and eerie connection, Crystal's appearance spurred the creation of Sky. Now she is here to take him back, like a witch who grants gifts and then revisits years later to claim something in return.

Molly shuts the photo album. She leans back in Jack's chair and closes her eyes. Baby Sky. Molly wanted him, she did, like she wanted all of her babies, but she had been so close to moving on and then there he was, a fifth baby, and she had already been so, so tired.

The next afternoon, Molly finds her Billie Holiday time tainted. She can't stand to be in her own house where people lurk in the yard whenever they want. She drives down the mountain to eat lunch at Suzy's Diner in town. She claims a large booth window seat all to herself. She eats a juicy blue cheese burger and plate of sweet potato fries, the local paper spread out before her. She feels restored. She thinks about popping in on Jack at the hardware store. She used to do it all the time; he loved the surprise, so why not? As she waits for change from the bill, she looks out the window and sees Crystal. She's waddling down the sidewalk with a crunched expression on her face, wearing the same stupid outfit as yesterday. She suddenly sits down on the curb in front of the hair salon across the street. Food lumps in Molly's gut.

Molly hasn't seen this girl in eighteen years and now here she is again, twice in two days, like a haunting. She watches Crystal thumb the keys on her cell phone and then throw the phone under a car parked nearby. The girl curls her shoulders and rests her elbows on her boney knees splayed out to make room for her belly. People walk by. No one stops to ask her if she's okay.

Molly wonders, what if Trish ever found herself pregnant, nearing delivery, and all alone? She'd want someone to help her daughter. She can't remember if Crystal's mother still lived here. She leaves a tip and crosses the street to the curb where Crystal is hunched and humming.

"Crystal, are you all right?" Molly asks.

Crystal looks up. Her eyes are bloodshot and swollen, her lips pale.

"What is it?" Molly squats in front of her.

"I'm sick. My stomach hurts, and I can't reach Sky. No one's picking up their fucking phone. The pain is ripping me in half."

Molly remembers the pain. "When are you due?"

"Two weeks." Crystal stretches her legs into the street.

"Two weeks? But, the classes just started last night."

"No, that's when Sky started." Crystal breathes harshly through her mouth.

"Does it feel good to do that? To breath like that?"

Crystal groans. "Get me out of this fucking body."

Molly arches her eyebrows. She wants to scold. She draws in a long breath. "Okay. Can you walk to my car? I'm driving you to the hospital down in Brattleboro. Should I call an ambulance?"

"I can walk."

"What about your phone."

"Fuck it. It's dead."

Molly hoists her purse over her shoulder. "Get up. Hold my arm. We'll get you to the car."

Inside the car, Molly helps Crystal with her seatbelt. She turns the key and a Billie Holiday CD plays, "I Cover the Waterfront."

Molly pulls out of the parking lot and makes her way through traffic willing the music to soothe the atmosphere. Crystal's quiet at first, then begins to hum. Molly looks at her. Crystal is like a child, her eyes closed, her lips in a pout.

"Do you like Billie Holiday?" Molly asks.

"I love her."

Molly stops at a light and reaches into her bag behind her seat for a water bottle. "Here, drink."

"But I already have to pee."

"You need to drink." Molly surprises herself with her maternal tone.

Crystal takes the bottle. "Can we hear that song again?" she asks.

Molly clicks the CD track arrow and settles into her seat. Billie Holiday's voice croons from the speaker. *I see the horizon, the great unknown. My heart has a name; it's as heavy as stone.* She could listen to that song all day.

Crystal drinks, sits up, and twists her spine into a stretch. "I'm better now."

"We'll go to the hospital anyway. Just to check," Molly says.

Crystal leans back in the seat.

Molly drives. A new song comes on; the tinkling of a piano and the slide of strings fill the car. *Lover man. Oh, where can you be?* Molly feels uncomfortable with these lyrics, considering Crystal may have been left. Where is her lover man? *Got a moon above me, but no one to love me.* Molly turns the volume down.

"I know you don't like me," Crystal says, eyes still closed. "You never did. You never wanted me anywhere near you."

Molly's not sure how to respond. She clutches the steering wheel.

"So, why are you helping me now?"

"I just am." Molly turns the up volume. "Let's not talk. Lean back and breathe."

Hush now don't explain. Just say you'll remain.

Molly wants to disappear into the music. She wants to swing and dip her hand outside of the car window. She wants to drop Crystal off at the hospital and drive all afternoon, east to the Maine coast, to the days when her family was everything and it was enough.

Molly turns into the hospital lot and parks near the entrance. She gets out and slams her door, leaving the engine running and Billie singing the blues. She strides to the other side of her car, opens the passenger door, and looks in at Crystal. "It's not that I don't like you. It's more that I don't know what I like."

Crystal nods, her face as pale as the beige vinyl seat. Billie's voice mimics a smoker's whine and it suddenly irritates Molly, how all Billie does in her songs is complain and change her mind. She reaches across Crystal, turns off the car, and grabs her keys.

"I'm going in with you." She unhitches Crystal's seatbelt as if Crystal is a toddler. "Bring the water."

Crystal follows Molly into the waiting room and does everything Molly tells her. When she whimpers, Molly tells her to breathe and sip water. When it's their turn, Molly leads Crystal to the examination room and stays through the tests.

"Your cervix is swollen," says the midwife. "But it's less than ten percent effaced." She looks at Molly. "Let's do an ultra-sound."

Molly sits beside Crystal as the midwife covers Crystal's belly with gel. When the sound of the heartbeat pulses through the room, Molly grabs Crystal's hand and squeezes. She stares at the screen. Molly still has the photos from every one of her five ultra-sounds during the first trimester, but has never seen the image of a near-term baby in utero. She presses a hand, fingers splayed, to her chest. The skin on the back of her neck prickles.

The midwife reviews the report. "False alarm. Go home and rest."

In front of the dilapidated colonial converted into affordable housing units where Crystal lives, Molly asks, "Do you have anyone who can come over?"

"My father's out-of-town."

"What about the baby's father?"

Crystal shakes her head. "Out of the picture." She gathers her bags.

"How did you get all the way up to our place yesterday?"

"You don't want to know."

"You hitched?"

Crystal opens the passenger door and swings her legs around to shimmy down to the sidewalk.

"Wait, Crystal, I have one more question." Molly focuses straight ahead at the cars parked along the street.

"Why did you choose Sky?" She knows it's not fair to stress Crystal anymore today, or to invade her son's privacy, but the question weighs more heavily than her shame in asking it.

"The truth? When I saw him at the career center, heard his name, I remembered you. I knew he'd be a good person." Crystal leans against the inside of the open door as if to prop herself up. "I remembered your whole family. I had fun at the beach. It was my first trip away from home." She smiles.

Molly realizes that except for Crystal's ukulele-playing grin in the kitchen yesterday and the wide-mouthed laugh with Sky in his truck, Molly hasn't seen Crystal look this content. She turns to face Crystal. She taps the steering wheel with her fingertips.

"I don't think I ever knew that," Molly says.

"Don't worry about Sky. He's my good luck charm. I won't cross any boundaries."

Molly nods. Sky turned out to be a kind, sensitive person, despite Molly's fatigue and flagging interest. He has a good head on his shoulders, knows how to act. And now Sky isn't the only one involved. Molly can help, too.

"Remember to drink water, no soda. Walk. Rest. Vitamins. Call us at home if you need us." Us. Molly likes the way that feels. "You have a landline in there?"

Crystal nods. "Thanks, Mrs. Ryan." Her voice sounds as thin and tired as Molly feels.

"Please, call me Molly."

That night, Molly can't sleep. Though her faith in Sky is restored, now she worries about Crystal. She hears the tinkling of ghost music in her head, wishes she could dance, wishes she could lose herself, fingers running along the keyboard of a piano. Even Wren's meditation tricks don't help. After tossing covers off and on and off again, she gets up and shuffles through the rooms of the house. In each room, she looks for something she loves and something she is ready to donate to the rummage sale down at Town Hall next month. If she moves some furniture, she can clear a space for a piano; it's time. Over breakfast, she'll talk it over with Jack. He'll encourage her. He always does and she knows this, and that they have been lucky.

She creeps into the master bedroom. Jack lies snoring on his side. Molly slips between the sheets. She scoots up next to the back of his body. She can smell his sleep sweat. He's always thrown off heat like a woodstove, and tonight, Molly feels cold on the inside and appreciates the warmth.

Jack makes a small sound in his throat. "Moll? Is that you?"

She likes that Jack calls her Moll. "Are you expecting someone else?" Even at midnight her whisper has a tone, that snarky marriage tone, yet she knows it is entirely forgivable.

He chuckles. She drapes her arm around his shoulder and splays her hand across his chest, feels the rhythm of his heart, but keeps her legs to herself. There's a chance for a great deal more loving between them. Maybe tomorrow. Maybe they'll dance in the living room, together, the way they used to in front of the kids all lined up on the couch in their clean pajamas. It could be a good thing.

Jack places his hand over hers. She hears his breath build back to a snore. What she would give to be able to sleep like that. To be able to sleep like that for days.

Wonder Woman

June 21, 8:30 a.m.
Every summer, the first Saturday after school lets out, I sail on my bike down the hill, three miles from our trailer, to the rummage sale at town center to collect junk for my projects. Last year I scored a girly bike for a dollar. I found a use for every piece of that rusted-up garbage and the bonus was this: I snagged a Wonder Woman lunch box, circa something or other. When I showed it to my mom she got all bouncy and Googled it. Turns out that it was an original, a collectible, worth a little money, but it's not for sale. When I'm home, working in what Mom calls my tinker shed, I like to take out the lunchbox and look at it. The picture of that super girl is something else. Pow! Like she's ready to kick the crap out of somebody. Now Mom gets the re-runs of Wonder Woman on DVD. She smiles her face off when we sit there on the couch together. She talks through the whole show, wondering what Lynda Carter is up to in her old age.

I'm working on a life-sized replica of Wonder Woman in 3-D out of chicken wire. Why? I'm obsessed. Maybe it's for my mom, but maybe it's for me. The main body's done, arms spread out, V for victory. I base the sculpture from the

picture on the lunch box. Yesterday when I was down here
helping Jack Ryan set up for the sale, I spotted a little trike.
I'm planning on grabbing that sucker before anyone else
sees it. The red metal is perfect for her super hero bra and
boots. The project is secret. When my mom tries to visit me
in the shed, she gets all three *Keep Out* signs in her face.

I'm a half hour early on purpose. I stash my new bike
from my Florida grandmother in the bushes on the far side
of the church across the post office parking lot, so no one
will think it's for sale. I promised I'd take care of this one.
I need it for basic transportation for my job mowing lawns.
I claim a spot in line on the handicap ramp with the other
early birds. There's time to relax a little. Look around. My
mom would call the sky June blue, saying that the new
leaves on the maples turn the volume up on color. I think
about this kind of shit sometimes, but I keep it to myself.
She talks about it enough for both of us. But it is the perfect
day. I feel lucky.

8:50 a.m.

Ten minutes before the opening of the sale. Here's Davey
and Jeremy. What a couple of idiots. I still have a bruise on
my shin from Davey's steel-toed boot. The asshole tripped
me on the bus on the last day of junior high. They get their
kicks hassling people, usually me. It's been this way since
my mom bought Davey's grandfather's trailer in a bank
sale two years ago. How's that my fault? Mom says Davey's
family has had their trouble and to be patient with him.
Great.

Jeremy's face is pale like it's made out of paper. Davey
stinks. Basically, they're stupid and ugly. Everybody can
look a little ugly when you get up close. Those two are ugly
from a distance.

I watch them hit the bake sale table across the yard in
front of the church. They buy up giant chocolate chip

cookies and stuff their faces. My stomach is hollow and gravelly. I forgot breakfast, so I crunch on a few peanuts stashed in my pocket from feeding the chickens this morning. The creeps are ignoring me now, but I know they have some sick plan up their sleeves. Jerks like them make me want to stay up on the hill in my shop, but I need the spokes from that little red trike. They'll be perfect for Wonder Woman's eyelashes. I check the clock on the church. Five minutes to go.

8:55 a.m.
Check it out. Melissa Wiley, ninth going into tenth, and hot, pushes through the line to meet up with her dad who's in front of me. She looks like her panties are in a bundle, pissed off, the usual. She picks at a scab above her elbow. She smells like peach pie with ice cream. I've got this eye-level view of her chest and one seriously tight shirt. Seriously. Right now, she's scowling at me. What? Doesn't she want me to gawk? Okay, so I try not to, but I can see the ribbed lines of the red fabric stretched full to capacity. I'd like to see Melissa Wiley in a Wonder Woman costume.

Right. What would a sophomore want with a freshman? Besides I don't have time for romance. I need to focus on my art. But here's Melissa wearing a necklace with a charm that she slips back and forth on the gold chain in the front where her top forms a perfect V for Victory! Pow! My eyes follow her knuckles back and forth. I'm like a crow around shiny objects and I'm trying to see what she's got between her fingers, I swear. Then she drops it, a silver charm that says HOPE. The HO is stacked on top of the PE and I laugh out loud because I'm thinking she doesn't even get that it says HO.

"What?" she snaps. She glares at me as she lifts her arms up to pull her honey hair off her shoulders. I'm looking from her armpits, to her mouth, to the necklace caught in her cleavage, and I can't stop. It's all right there. Even up close, Melissa Wiley is not one-bit ugly.

"Nothing," I say. I hold my hands up like I'm about to get frisked by a cop. What? Like I'm going talk about the HO in front of her dad.

"You little perv. Get the hell away from me."

My mother would say that girl's got a mouth on her. Her Dad's talking to the couple in front of them. I turn and squint at the people at the end of the line. I'm not budging from my early bird spot.

Jeremy and Davey climb up the stairs on the outside of the iron railing and slide down like they're eight-year-olds. They eye me the whole time, holding back on an assault in front of the grown-ups. They said everything they needed to on the bus the last day of school before summer vacation: how they know I always buy up the old bikes, how they plan to get them first and have their dads put them in their trucks, so I don't try to steal them. Like I'm the kind of person who steals things. Those jerks are lying about the bikes to bug me. They're only allowed to look around anyway. I know their moms don't want any junk coming back to their houses; I've heard them say it. Besides, Davey's dad is in jail, but I didn't call him out on that.

It's the same every summer, their stupid games. The clock on the church strikes nine and the crowd starts pushing us from behind. The creeps run off. I'm in.

9:00 a.m.

Inside Town Hall, rummagers rush around the "Treasures" area. I slip in and out of bodies between tables crowded with glass jars and broken toys, through the room, and out the back door to the Carriage House stalls which displays the outdoor junk. Melissa is already out back, poking around the used fish tanks. Jeremy and Davey are here, too, testing out the old bikes. I can't believe it. They ran around the back of the building and crawled under the split-rail fence.

When they see me, Davey starts ooh-ing and ahh-ing over the red trike that's displayed next to a yellow and black plastic one. He's acting like the old red trike's a goddamn Corvette. He yells, "Hey, Rory. Look at this sweet little trike. I'm checking it out for my baby sister. Maybe you two could go out."

Real funny. But, oh yeah, that's right, he can't help being a dickhead. I flip him off. Did he figure out that the red trike is the one I'm here for, or is he just randomly messing with me?

Jeremy's more interested in Melissa who squats down to sort through the equipment in a tank. The waist of her shorts has ridden low and a lacey strip of pink underwear dips beneath the top of her butt crack. I admit it. Jeremy's got excellent taste. He looks like he's about to pass out dead. I walk over to the plastic bike and examine it like it's the Holy Grail.

"Fuck," Melissa hisses. Her face is bent into the tank. She's pulling on her hair. It's tangled up in the electrical cord on a water pump. The jerks just stand there, so I walk over and squat down next to her.

I fiddle with her hair and the cord. Her neck is slick with sweat. She's breathing fast. I free her. "Got it," I say.

She stands. Her eyes are misted over, but sharpen up in seconds. "Thanks, you little shit. Now quit following me around."

I'm still squatting and there's my face, right at crotch level, my nose about a foot from the snap on her shorts. There's a strip of sunburn where the hem meets her thighs. Butterflies stitched in gold are flying on her pockets. She shoves my forehead with the butt of her palm and I fall back on my ass. Okay, I totally deserved that. Davey howls. Melissa sashays over to him by the red trike. She's smirking.

She runs her fingers through the tassels on the end of a handlebar, and I know we're all wishing we could be the trike.

"Wait, this is my tricycle," she yells. "My mother's selling my tricycle!"

Douche 1 and Douche 2 back away. I stand up.

Melissa runs her hands all along the trike, the shiny chrome and the creamy leather seat, like a girl in the movies would rub the arms and shoulders of a guy, like she's feeling for something on his skin. Melissa rips the price sticker off the seat, rolling it up between her fingers. She flicks it to the ground. She puts her hand on her chest, in the way she does, to play with the necklace, but it's not there. She spins around, glares at me. "What did you do with it, creep?"

"What?" I squawk.

"My fucking necklace, the one you kept staring at." Then she squats to search the ground around the bike and the fish tank. Her hair's covering her face, but I think she might be crying. "You took it."

Mr. Wiley walks over and says, "Get up off the ground, Melissa. What is going on?"

She springs up. "My necklace, the one I got from Shawn before he left, it's missing. That's what. And these little creeps are giving me shit. I can't wait to get out of this fucking town."

"Watch your mouth, Melissa," says Mr. Wiley.

Her hair is all around her face now. Some of it sticks to the wetness on her cheeks, which are patchy and pink. She throws an arm out to point at the little red trike. "And that's my bike."

I feel bad. The brother who gave her the necklace, Shawn, is stationed in Afghanistan. I keep my head down and scuff up some gravel. Jeremy and Davey creep backwards and slip over the fence. As usual, they act like a couple of dudes until shit hits the fan, then they run. I just want to get the red trike, grab another older kid bike I see, and head home to work in my shed.

"First things first." Mr. Wiley drops his hand on my shoulder. "Can you help us out about the necklace, Rory?"

"No. Really, I don't know anything. I just wanted to buy the trike." I wonder if my mom is here with the station wagon, and if she's looking for me.

Melissa knocks her dad's hand off my shoulder. "It's not for sale." Then she glares at her father. "I'm taking it home. And I want that aquarium."

She yanks the trike behind her, heads to the door leading back into the Town Hall, though today, it's only supposed to be an exit. But no one's going to bust her for that.

Mr. Wiley shakes his head. "Teenage girls. One minute they're sweet little bunnies and the next, well, get the hell out of their way. You know what I mean?"

This kind of question isn't something I'm supposed to know how to answer, so I just shrug my shoulders and look around.

"See you later, Rory." He picks up the aquarium and follows Melissa.

I wave. I grab the other bike I want, the shitty one, and wheel it out to pay Sky Ryan who's taking money at a table on the lawn. Across the parking lot at the church bake sale table, I wolf down a couple of brownies. I can hear Melissa. She's over at the post office, in the parking lot, laughing her head off. She's watching Davey the Douche walk on his hands while Jeremy holds up his legs. Davey's shirt is flipped over his face and he's screaming that he can't see. What a couple of tools. Hard to believe they made it out of middle school.

Davey falls over and brings Jeremy down with him and they roll around on the pavement. Melissa seems to be all done laughing and glances around like she's bored with these guys and looking for something better. She sees me

staring at her and flips me off. Davey and Jeremy get up.
All three of them stand there talking and flipping me off,
but I try to act like I could care less. My mom pulls up,
parks, and gets out of the car. I tell her about the trike and
show her the consolation prize, another broken down piece
of rusted crap. She laughs. We poke through some garden
stuff on the lawn sale. The whole time, I'm ready to head
back up the hill. Mom will have to drive the old bike home.
It won't be easy getting it into her car. When she's ready, I
go to get my new bike out of the bushes, but it isn't where
I left it. I glance over at Davey and Jeremy. They're
slobbering all over Ms. Wade, the art teacher we used to
have in K-3 and will have again next year. They're probably
brown-nosing her all up.

My mom and I look everywhere for the bike. No luck.
No goddamn fucking luck. She talks to Jack Ryan who's in
charge. He and Sky help us make a few posters that Mom
and I tacked to telephone poles around town center. I sure
don't want to be the one to explain this to my grandmother.

1:00 p.m.
Back home, I visit the chickens, scrawny bastards just like
me. My favorite is the spunky game hen. I call her Little
One. She's an anarchist. She refuses to live in the coop with
the other girls, but somehow she survives the nights. She
sleeps in some dirt in a clay flowerpot on a stump next to
my shed. I worry about her, but I also want her to live how
she wants to live. I feed her peanuts and scratch her head.
She likes it. I like it. She follows me into my work shed.

I look at the Wonder Woman lunch box and then check
over the crap bike that I managed to ride home. There are
a few good parts. The white plastic seat can be cut up for
the stars on Wonder Woman's blue panties. The spokes
can be cut down for her lashes. I took a piece of some
shiny gold fabric from Mom's pile of sewing tidbits for the

belt. Then I notice something. I look up at my Wonder Woman towering over half of a foot taller than me, the same as Melissa Wiley.

I hear my mother's voice talking on the phone as she walks towards the shed. "Rory," she calls.

The chickens in the yard start squawking like they're on watch duty. I stash the gold cloth and the lunch box under the workbench.

"I'm coming out."

She stands there with the portable phone, covering the mouthpiece. It's probably my grandmother. She hands me the phone. Time to 'fess up about the missing bike. If only I can stall because I'm sure as hell going to get to the bottom of the missing bike.

"Hello," I mumble.

"Rory?"

It's a girl's voice, one that I don't recognize. Why would I? No girl ever called my house before.

"Yeah."

"Hey, it's Melissa."

What the hell does she want? I clear my throat. "Hey."

"I need to talk to you. I'll be awake when you come to mow over at the Stewart's in the morning. I'll meet you on the front porch."

How does she know my mowing schedule? But I don't ask. My mom's standing there pretending to look over the garden. I turn my back to her and take a few steps in the other direction. "Why? What's up?" But, the line goes dead. I pause. "Okay, sure, bye," I say to the dial tone so that my mom doesn't know that Melissa just hung up on me.

"Who was that?" Mom asks.

"Melissa Wiley."

"Oh. Jim Wiley's daughter."

"Yeah." I head back towards the shed and see Little One waiting for me on the windowsill. I turn around and say,

"See ya later, Mom." I know that look on her face. She wants to hang out. Wants to know what's going on, so I leave the door open. The three *Keep Out* signs seem a little harsh. She already knows I don't like her around when I'm out here. "Let's watch a couple of episodes tonight, okay?" I call out.

She nods and wanders back to the trailer, stops to sniff the honeysuckle bush by the house, taking her sweet time. I pick up Little One, tickle her head feathers, and wonder what Melissa Wiley wants. She probably still thinks I have her goddamn necklace. Little One looks at me with her quick shiny eyes, like she can hear what I'm thinking. I set her down. She pokes around under the bench and pulls at the gold fabric I bought at the sale. I cut off a piece for her and stash the rest on a shelf up high. Chickens are simple. Little One scratches at her scrap while I work on finishing the curvy legs of my wire lady. When I'm working, I can get completely out of my head.

June 22, 8:00 a.m.
The next morning, I wake up. I feel a twist in my gut. I have my lawn mowing jobs in town, but something else, too. Melissa. I feed the hens in the coop. Little One struts around my mother's garden.

"Hey, Little. Made it through another night, didn't ya, girl?" I toss her a couple of peanuts. Then I remember my missing bike. After a few bangs with a hammer I can get the rummage sale bike to ride straight. I realize I'll look like an ass, but it's a ride.

When I get to Melissa's house, she's a no show. It's probably all just a big joke and Davey and Jeremy put her up to it. Figures I'd fall for it. I'm about to leave when I hear a whistle. It's Melissa. She beckons me from the back end of the driveway that separates her house from the Stewart's. She's wearing a black sports bra and a pair of Hello Kitty pajama bottoms and no shoes. She's holding on to the handle of my birthday bike. Dr. Stewart comes out to the front porch to water the geraniums with his little boy, Elliot. Dr. Stewart waves. We wave back. The kid gawks at us. Cute kid. Melissa jerks her head towards the backyard. What? Am I stupid enough to follow her? I guess so.

When I join her in the back, I notice the skin under her eyes is grayish-blue. It's smudged make-up. She's been crying again. Her lips are pale. I've heard people say it's hard to be a teenage girl. She pulls me closer by my arm and hisses in my ear, "Shh. I don't want my parents to know about this."

I can smell her breath, rank from sleeping, and catch a whiff of armpit odor. The smell of muffins baking is coming from the kitchen window at the Stewarts. I forgot to eat breakfast again.

"Thanks for helping me with my hair at the sale yesterday. Those fuck-ups talked me into thinking you stole my necklace. They told me they took your bike from the bushes and asked if I wanted revenge. I don't know why I listened."

I knew those freaks were behind it. I shrug. "Whatever."

"This summer is already so fucking boring. I was just going to keep it until you gave me back the necklace." She's whispering and a small drop of her spit splashes on her chin. I feel like rubbing it off, but I'm holding up the rummage sale bike. Besides, I'd never have the balls to touch Melissa Wiley. Never in a million years.

"You didn't take my necklace, did you?" she asks.

Before I can tell her no, someone opens a window on the second floor of her house and we hear the radio announcer giving the Eye on the Sky weather report. She grabs my wrist and pulls me closer. I feel her chest press against my arm. Dr. Stewart calls over, "You mowing today, Rory?"

"Be right there."

I have to go, but I like feeling her against my arm. I shut my eyes. I didn't know Melissa's boobs would be soft like this.

"Do you have it?" she asks.

"I swear I don't know anything about the necklace." I sound like I have a sore throat. "I gotta go."

"Here. Take your fucking bike." She croaks these words in my ear and thrusts the handlebars into my gut. "Tell on us if you want." Then suddenly she lets go of my wrist and disappears into her house.

I'm standing behind her father's truck holding onto two bikes with my skinny pecker stiff in my gym shorts. Evelyn Stewart comes out to her back porch and shakes out a dust cloth. She looks nothing like my mom. She dresses up, wears lipstick and high heels at the bank where she works. She waves her white rag at me to say hello and walks back inside. She's probably been watching us the whole time from her kitchen window.

When I finally get the mowing done and push both bikes three miles up the hill to home, I tell Mom that my missing bike was found in a ditch in the stream behind the post office. A prank. She pulls me in for a hug, which feels super weird after Melissa.

What a goddamn start to summer vacation.

A week later, 12:00 p.m.

Mom cleans houses. She's busiest in the summers and I'm just fine with that. I keep my shop door open. I've got the skeleton of my sculpture woman finished and I bought some red and blue and gold spray paint. I don't know why I didn't think of that before. It's like I enjoy making things harder for myself. I'll shape sheet aluminum into clothes and paint it.

Wonder Woman will be see-through everywhere but where her clothes go. Chicken wire wrapped around and around on itself creates a random layered effect. I like it. So far, she's bald and looks like an alien. I'm waiting for inspiration on how to deal with the hair. I need a thick, black mane for her gold headband. She'll need to look good up close and from far away.

It's lunchtime and Little One has yet to show up for her peanuts. Come to think of it, I haven't seen the squirt all day. I put away my tools and step out into the yard. The sky is layered with gray clouds. Plastic seedling trays fly around in the garden. It looks like the black and white scenes from *The Wizard of Oz*. I go inside the trailer for a new bag of peanuts, hoping that if I crinkle the plastic Little One will appear. I'm out in the yard calling for a chicken when Melissa Wiley revs it into my driveway on her brother Shawn's ATV. She's breaking every law in the book, driving an off-road vehicle without a license.

She cuts the motor and hops off. She's wearing a purple bikini top under a skimpy white shirt and a pair of low pink shorts. She flips her hair loose from a bun and lifts her arms to make a ponytail with the rubber band from her wrist. Her belly button's newly pierced. I can't help looking at it and she rolls her eyes. As she walks up to me, dust swirls in storm winds around us both, but I notice she's wearing her *HOPE* necklace with a shiny new silver chain. She thrusts her chest forward.

"Found it!"

"Cool." I don't know what else to say.

"It was at the bottom of that fish tank. The chain broke. I'm here to make an official apology."

She actually seems happy. She walks towards the chicken coop and I follow, catching up to walk with her, wondering what the hell she'll do next, if she'll bust into my shed.

"Where are you going?" I ask.

"I had to get out of that fucking house. We got a phone call from Shawn last night and my mother's turning the dining room upside down, polishing all the silver and washing the china. Why? I have no idea. It's not like he's coming home for dinner." She flicks a loose shoulder strap back in place. "Want to go for a ride on the muster field?"

"Me?" This squeaks out before I can stop it.

"Why not?" She squints and folds her arms under her boobs. "Well, no one else is around this summer. Besides, girls are bitches."

The old muster field is five miles from our trailer. To get there you have to go down the hill through town center. My legs feel weak and my hands sweat. If I don't go, we're headed into my shop. If I go, we could get seriously caught.

I lunge in front of her to block the opening of my shed. "I think it might rain," I say, sounding lame as shit. I'm still holding the bag of peanuts, now crushed against my stomach. "Want to see my room?"

She raises her eyebrows. "You are a little perv, aren't you?" She flicks her strap again. "No, I love the wind. I want to ride." She stretches her arms, clasps her hands together over her head, and flips them around so her palms are facing the sky. Her belly is smooth and tan, the color of a perfect pancake. The wind blows wisps of her hair into her face. She looks like somebody in a movie. I feel that telltale tightening in my pants. Her eyes glance beyond my shoulder. She smiles and moves past me towards the shed.

"Wait!" I yell.

"Awwwwww," she sings.

Little One is hunched up on the windowsill, her feathers standing on end from the wind. She hops down and struts inside through the open door like she owns the place. Melissa follows the chicken. I follow Melissa. I'm having a quiet fit.

"She is so cute. Can I hold her?" Melissa picks up Little One. She presses the bird to the side of her face.

I stand in front of my wire woman covering about two-thirds of the body. Melissa cradles my chicken in her arms like it's a baby. The stupid game hen is completely relaxed, as if hypnotized by the strokes on her chest, her scrawny feet stuck straight in the air. Melissa is cooing like a dove. She's completely turned to mush over a chicken.

"Is she yours?"

"Yeah." I shift my weight to cover more of the sculpture. "We have a whole flock of crazy breeds in the coop. My mom raises them for the fair. This one is mine. Want to see them?"

"Maybe, later." She rocks Little One back and forth. "I want a kitten but my mom is allergic. My dad says we'll keep asking until she gives in. I'll keep her in my room and in three years I'm out of here anyway."

"Where are you going?"

Her face changes from sweetie pie to bitch in seconds. "How the hell should I know?" Her voice sounds choked. "Some city somewhere. Anywhere but here."

I wonder what's wrong with here. Stark Run is what I know, how the sky turns gray in winter, how the river rushes in spring. I'd miss how the night sky lights up with stars. I've been to the city, Boston, on a field trip. I couldn't breathe right. I'm about to argue my point when Little One squirms and scratches Melissa's arm. She flings the bird to the floor.

"Jeez!" I yell.

"Well, sorry, but she messed me up." The old Melissa is back. Little One runs out of the shed. I watch through the open door as she crawls under the henhouse. Melissa examines the scratch, twisting her arm against her chest. She sucks blood from the inside of her upper arm. I don't move. I've got to get Melissa completely outside before she sees Wonder Woman.

"Nasty little beast." She studies me with her arms across her chest. I still can't figure out why she's stayed this long. She's already apologized.

"Do you want to wash those scratches?" I ask. Then rain lets loose from the summer sky and pounds the metal roof. "Let's make a run for the trailer," I yell.

"Not a chance." She sees a torn old school bus seat in the corner by my desk and plops down. "I'm waiting right here and keep that door open. Is your mother home?" Then her face lights up and she stands again. "What is *that?*"

I back away. Her mouth forms the shape of a bagel hole as she circles my statue. Just as I suspected, the two ladies are exactly the same height. Now Melissa is smiling, but it's not mean. "This is incredible. Where'd you get it?"

I shrug.

"Did you make it?" She smacks the front of my shoulder knocking me off balance.

I nod, frowning.

"Shut up." She walks around it again and starts looking through all of my crap. I stand by the door, hoping my mom gets here soon so I can tell Melissa I have to go.

"You total weirdo," she says, her mouth round with what I think could be a small amount of awe. "What's it going to be?"

I feel a little stupid. I don't want to say Wonder Woman. "It's not supposed to be anything."

"But, it is! Look. It's a girl, isn't it? Very sexy, Rory Tree. You're more of a little pervert than I thought." She ruffles my hair and I feel like a jerk.

"I'm just messing around."

"Nice work. I'm serious." She flops back down on the bus seat. "You're an *artiste.* Is this like your own private hideout or something? This place is so cool."

"I like it here." That sounds dumb. I edge towards the door, ready for her to go.

"Relax, Tree. I'm not going to tell anyone about your sex toy." She snorts.

I shake my head. "Whatever."

She giggles, then leans back and crosses her arms over her head, closes her eyes. The word HOPE rests silver and flat against tanned skin. It rises and falls with her breathing. She's quiet for a long time. Her mouth pulled tight, like she's holding something in. I look out the window. The rain stops as quickly as it started.

"It's nice up here, Rory." She sounds sleepy. "It's peaceful."

I stare at her lips, now relaxed. "I never thought about it. I just live here, me, and my mom."

Her eyes fly open and she sits up. "Why do you think Jeremy hangs out with Davey? He's at least a little decent. But, Davey, Jesus, what a tool." She brings up the gruesome twosome as if they are already part of a conversation. "When they came by my house with your bike that day of the sale, Davey said I had to meet him in the park for a hand job lesson. He said I owed him. What's wrong with people?"

I don't really know, so I keep my mouth shut. Then she leans forward, presses her forehead against her knees. Her arms droop to the sides and she starts to cry. Shit. Again. I look around for a tissue, but all I can find is the scrap of gold cloth I gave to Little One. It's not too gnarly, so I hand it to her and ask, "Why do you cry so much?" Brilliant.

She looks up. Her face is hot pink. "I don't know." She whines, sounding like a little girl. Then, she yells, "Because I hate everything and everybody! The whole fucking universe!"

We both listen as the sound waves bounce around the walls of the shed. I scuff my sneaker against the dirt floor while she wipes up her face. Melissa is about the first kid I've met who makes any sense. She speaks up. Admits it when she's been an idiot. Besides being hot, she's badass. She's in *my* shed. We're alone. Sort of. With Wonder Woman looming it's like there are three of us. I try to think about something else besides the way I can see Melissa's bikini through her tank top. I'm too young for this.

I think about how I should head down to the dump now that the air has cooled off to see if anything interesting came into the metal department since last week. I'm about to open my mouth, say I'll go three-wheeling if she'll take me to the dump, when a car drives up. Great. It's Mom.

We walk out to the driveway. It's not Mom. It's Davey's mom and she's getting out of the car. Davey and Jeremy get out, too. They're laughing silently behind her back, pointing and jeering at Melissa and me. Davey thrusts his pointer finger in and out of a hole he makes with his other hand. He's a real mature guy.

"Hello, Rory. I'm looking for Shannon," says Davey's mom. "I'm working for the census. Is she home?"

"Nope. She's at work. She'll be home any minute." Davey's mom looks like she could use some supper and a good night's sleep. The guys start kicking around an empty seedling tray. Little One struts over and I realize I still have the bag of peanuts in my left hand. All this time, I'm clutching the bag of peanuts like it's a life ring.

Melissa leans over and picks up the chicken, tucking Little One's legs and feet carefully between her arm and hip like it's a toddler, like she does it every day. I feed Little One some peanuts from my hand and she coos. I rub the feathers below her beak. I'm careful not to touch the side of Melissa's boob.

"Awwww," Melissa says. "Look, you guys." Her face is bright and happy, like we're all best friends.

Davey's mom smiles and says, "Why don't you tell your mother that I stopped by, Rory. I'll come back another day. Get back in the car, boys."

Davey and Jeremy walk back to the car pretending to kiss and hug. Behind his mother's back, Davey tries to pretend hump Jeremy, but Jeremy shoves him off. He keeps looking back, wiggling his butt and sticking out his chest.

When they turn around to watch us out the back window of the car Melissa flips them off with her free hand.

"Fuckheads," she says to me. She sets Little One down, carefully this time. "I should go. My mom doesn't know I left with the four-wheeler. She'll freak."

She straddles the seat of the ATV and starts it up. "Later, Rory."

I feel another tug in my shorts and drop the bag of peanuts to hide any obvious evidence. I wave. She spins out. Little One pulls on the bag of peanuts as I watch Melissa ride away. Between Melissa and those assholes my stomach's in knots and my chest feels like I just finished riding my bike up hill. I look around the place—our trailer, the garden, and the chickens in the pen stalking bugs. All's quiet now and the sky is what my Mom calls post-rain gorgeous.

July 7, 10:00 a.m.
Another week of summer goes by and I haven't worked much on my wire girl. I've made some drawings, tried to plan for her hair, but every sketch turns out to look more like Melissa than Wonder Woman. Some people wouldn't notice, but I'm not stupid.

When I'm not doing yard work in town, I spend more time on our neighbor's property, the far end of the Ryan's mountain farm, walking the trails of their sugarbush or just lying down in the grass at the edge of the hayfield. Sometimes I hear the horses or Sky Ryan's pickup truck. It needs a new muffler. Mostly it's quiet around here. Grasshoppers. Birds. Most kids my age hightail it to the pool down at the rec center, but I can't swim very well, and I've got the East Branch of Stark Run snaking right past our yard for dipping. I'd rather stay up here.

Today, I watch one cloud chase after another. It's never going to catch up. It'd be like me going after Melissa. The more days that pass, the more I wonder if her visit was a fluke.

I make a promise to myself: get focused on the sculpture, start working on the clothes, or look for a better job than mowing. My mom's out cleaning houses and I'm just fucking around most of the time. When I head back to the trailer to grab a sandwich, I see a census packet hanging from the doorknob. Where'd that come from? Mrs. Morgan must have come looking for my mother again while I was out in the field. People in Stark Run barge in whenever they feel like it. Maybe that's why Melissa wants out, for a little privacy. I hear you can get lost in a city.

I hope those jerk bags didn't come and mess with my stuff or scare the chickens. I scan the yard for Little One, though it's not her snack time. It's not unusual for her to be out and about. I check on Mom's chickens. They're all accounted for but not Little One. I'm heading out to look in my shed when the phone rings in the kitchen and I run inside to answer it.

"Hello."

"It's Melissa."

My stomach flips. I grip the edge of the kitchen counter. "Oh, hey."

"I think you should come down here as soon as you can." Her voice sounds like it's tied up in knots.

"What's up?"

"Rory, just come over. Like now."

The phone clicks. Dial tone. Whatever she wants, it's bound to be better than staring at the goddamn clouds.

10:30 a.m.

I fly down the hill to Melissa's house. When I arrive, she's sitting on the steps of her front porch wearing a yellow dress without straps and I notice bright white tan lines on her shoulders from her bikini top. Her feet are bare. She's holding a baby blue towel bundled on her lap. She's quiet and sniffling, and I think, here we go again. I lean my bike against a tree and sit down next to her.

"What's up?" I ask.

I look down at the towel as she unfolds it and see Little One lying there, eyes closed, neck twisted in an odd position, legs stiff. Melissa carefully places the bird in the towel onto my lap. I stroke my chicken's head. There's a speck of blood on her beak.

There isn't room for air in my throat. I close my eyes. I feel my body start to shake. I don't understand how Little One is here on my lap on this porch, or how it came to be that Melissa Wiley is hugging and rocking me, noises coming from my throat that sound like someone else's, my face wet with snot. I think of Mom, but I smell lemons and butter and Mom's scent is bleach. I'm in the arms of Melissa Wiley in broad daylight. I feel her softness. I pull myself together. Clear my throat. Melissa lets me go and I straighten. I open my eyes.

"She was on my porch when I came out to check for mail. I'm expecting a letter from Shawn." Her back is straight and her hands are folded on her lap. She looks and sounds like a rich lady or a teacher. "But, I don't know how or why Little One got to be here; I swear. Do you believe me?"

In my head, I flash on the census packet on the knob of the trailer door. The thing I can't figure out is how Davey got a chicken past his mother and into the car. That guy must be so much more twisted than I thought. I want to puke. I'm afraid I'll lose it again.

"I believe you."

I gather up the bundle. I get up and leave without saying good-bye.

12:00 p.m.

I walk the road up the hill to our place, holding Little One's body in the towel against my chest, but except for the cries of kids screaming at the pool, and wondering if Davey and Jeremy are jerking around over there, I don't remember any of it.

In the shed, I wrap her rigid body with the gold cloth that she liked and take her and a shovel through the woods and out into the Ryan's field to a shady spot under an old apple tree. Now, while I dig a grave, I hear the sound of the ATV coming up the hill and I know that it's Melissa, but I keep going, sweat tickling my temples and neck. The engine gets louder as she gets closer and then stops. In a few minutes, I hear her call my name.

It's funny. I don't mind any more that she might be making herself at home in my shed, rummaging through my stuff. I take my time. I cover my little chicken with dirt and replace the grass. I'm careful to cover the grave with a rock so a coy dog won't dig her up. As I work, I figure something else out, too. It's all over for Davey and Jeremy. I'm done. I've got Melissa Wiley on my side. Between the two of us, we'll think of a way to put them in their places. Sorry, Mom, but nice Rory is no more.

After the burial, I stand and stretch and look up at the sky. There's not one cloud, just solid blue, like in an enhanced picture on a Vermont wall calendar that tourists buy. There's a breeze. A bumblebee lands on a dandelion near my feet and I watch how still it becomes. I think of Melissa, the way she was sitting on the steps in that yellow dress, the tan lines, her hair. I head back to the yard.

As I approach the shed, I see the ATV where my mom usually parks her dumpy old Forester at the end of the day. Outside of the shed is the little red trike from the rummage sale. How the hell did she get that thing up here driving an ATV? Then I realize I left my new bike at her house. Damn.

Melissa's inside like I knew she would be. She's humming. I walk in. She's sitting on the bus seat, her yellow dress spread out around her like she's at a picnic. She's taken the sketches from my desk and spread them on the dirt floor in front of her feet and now we're both looking at the way I really see her. Sure, I play up her body, the belly button ring, the curves, but in all of the drawings, her face is lit up like the day, the shape of her hair, soft pencil strokes the color of honey bringing out the fire in her eyes. But it's her mouth that I got perfect, those lips ready to rant or pucker into sadness or open up for a laugh; you just never know. The sketches snap and spark off everything she's got going on inside. I can feel it.

She looks up at me. Grins. Then, she stands, smoothing out the front of her dress. But she doesn't come any closer and I hope to hell one of us will know what to say and do.

"You okay?" she asks.

I nod.

She holds her arms out, not up over her head like the sculpture, but down near her hips, her palms turned up. She's asking another question now, a different question. I step towards her. She's beautiful and calm.

Deep End

Too many kids bobbled and raced in the cloudy over-chlorinated water that Saturday afternoon for anyone to notice that Jillanna's tiny brother, Elliot, had stumbled in over his head. The crush of swimmers included Jillanna, who, on most hot days, played Marco Polo until her eyes burned and her fingertips bled from hanging on the concrete lip of the pool. The lifeguard had climbed down from his stand to spritz Bactine on Jillanna's puckered scrapes. Someone's mother screamed.

Jillanna turned to see her friends humped and hanging on the side in the deep end, their shoulders pink from the high sun, their faces pale with horror. They reminded her of shrimp cocktail clinging to a bowl and she laughed at the image in her head, even when she knew that whatever was happening wasn't funny.

From where she stood at the lifeguard stand, she scanned the lawn area on the other side of the shallow end. Her eyes focused on her mother who was holding Elliot to the side of her face, his chest against her ear, his head cocked like a rag doll. Two pale limp legs dangled from his Superman swim trunks. Her mother's expression crumpled and she felt her heart clench. A different lifeguard pried

Elliot away from her mother. A group of women surrounded the scene, blocked Jillanna out.

The sound of an ambulance from the fire department grew until Jillanna could feel the screeching vibration inside her chest. She looked down at her fingertips. The sting of the antiseptic was the last feeling she could remember for weeks to come.

The sweltering days of July trudged into August. The funeral over, Jillanna's father had gone back to work. He was a therapist. He helped people. He had to move on and he had said all of this to Jillanna with his hands on her shoulders. She remembered how heavy they felt, the weight of his hands.

She spent time sitting beside her mother on the scratchy brown couch in the living room. Neighbors from in town and friends who lived up the mountain visited, grown-ups. At first, Jillanna suffered through the weeping, and then found it interesting, the way her mother's friends twisted the shapes of their faces to match her mother's, smiled when she smiled, sunk their quivering mouths into a container for the next round of tears. Through all of the dabbing of faces, Jillanna was in charge of moving the Kleenex box from one woman to the next. But after days of this, the condolences became more and more faint to her as she grew restless cooped up in the house. Sentiments like, *we will never know why something like this could have happened* and *there is simply no explanation for such a horror* trilled through the room like the tinny chime of the brass clock on the mantel that punctuated the dull hours.

Jillanna knew the reason. It was simple. Blistering temperatures had sent everyone to the pool. Kids swarmed. No one had been paying attention. No one. Including that lifeguard. Elliot had been as invisible then as he was now. But of course she couldn't say anything about that out loud.

Day after day, she watched as her mother shuffled toward the ringing doorbell, the sympathetic friends and their foiled plates of food, as if assurances could save them all from suffocating with guilt. At the end of each afternoon, Jillanna cleaned up the used tissues, plucking up white wads. Once she found one that was streaked with red lipstick, reminding her of the blood from her fingertips on the gauze that day at the pool.

In the time between visitors, Jillanna shadowed her mother through rooms of the house made dim by closed curtains. She hardly spoke for fear that her questions would split her mother apart. Sometimes Jillanna coughed into the gloom to test her voice, to snatch at her mother's attention; she wasn't the only kid in the world who ever bothered a lifeguard for First Aid. But her mother just paced, eyes straight ahead. She quit her job at the bank to become a zombie in her own house.

Now and then, Jillanna expected to see Elliot run down the hall, a toy airplane in hand, his lips sputtering busy motor sounds, spittle flying. Elliot had made her mother laugh. He made them all laugh, a cute kid, the kind you see in magazine ads for cereal.

Jillanna only broke from her mother's side to eat ice cream on the back porch with her father after dinner, enjoying the cool burn at the back of her throat, the nerve freeze that shimmied to her brain. At night, she slept alone in her room. There, she dreamt of clear blue water, shallow and lapping on white sand. In tidal pools, among crusted rocks, she saw her mother's feet, the pearl polish of her mother's toenails pebble-like among stones. Beside them were Elliot's chubby white feet wavering in water and sunlight like tiny sea anemones. Jillanna searched, looking for her own feet, the polish on her own toes, and woke when she could not find them. She'd lie awake until morning wondering if she, or any of them, could ever be happy again.

One morning, with little summer left before school began, the air in the house felt sluggish from heat and the different scents that came in from the skin of outsiders: soap, sunscreen, herbal bug spray. Though the number of visitors had dwindled, a few women still floated in and out of the room with the dust. Pleasantries limped along. How many ways could they make excuses for what had happened to Elliot? Jillanna ached for one of them to tell the truth.

As she sat next to her mother on the brown couch, she tried to remember a normal summer day. She longed for friends, afternoons spent at the pool, and the soothing beams of sunlight that soaked their backs when they stretched out on their tummies, the sides of their faces pressed to the hot cement. She missed the sound of Elliot's troll-like voice mimicking pop songs from the kitchen radio while she set the table. He got the words all wrong. But mostly, she missed the life she used to have, and that made her want the things she wanted even more. She felt the weight inside her chest push against her lungs, in the way she felt when attempting to blow into a tight party balloon. Desire coupled with the dense air in her throat, forming a clump of words that exploded.

"It was not my fault!" Jillanna shouted into a thick pause in the ladies' conversation.

Her mother's friends set down their teacups or brushed crumbs from their laps. They would not meet her gaze as she sought their confirmation. Jillanna's mother wrapped her arm around Jillanna's shoulders, pulling her close and stroking her temple too hard. The clasp of her mother's charm bracelet tugged a wisp of hair on the base of Jillanna's neck, skin pulled tight by her ponytail. It caused a sharp repetitive sting that, strangely, Jillanna enjoyed; at least her mother was touching her again.

"You're right about that, Jillanna," said Meredith Wade from the floral high-back chair that blocked the window. "It was no one's fault."

Meredith Wade was the young art teacher, who the kids all loved, who lived in her dead mother's house at the other end of town. She was pretty. It was the first time she ever visited. From across the carpet, Meredith Wade looked into Jillanna's eyes. "I know you miss your brother. We are all very sad, but it is absolutely no one's fault."

Jillanna pulled away from her mother. She nodded, but the problem was she did not miss her brother as much as she thought she should. She remembered that he had cried in the night as a baby, waking her up, and that her parents had hissed at each other in the room next door. She had made drizzle castles for him to destroy last summer in his sand pile out back. She liked the way the droopy ears of his fuzzy wolf cub hat bounced up and down as he struggled to walk in deep snow in winter. Sometimes she pushed him around the neighborhood in the stroller to give her mother a break, but other than that, Jillanna hardly spent any time with Elliot. She went to school and played with friends her own age.

Earlier in the summer, when her mother offered her rides home from the pool after work, Jillanna chose to walk, preferring the open air to the stuffy car and the smell of daycare peanut butter smeared on her little brother's car seat. She didn't really know him. She should have taken those rides in the car. Maybe he hadn't been gone long enough for her to truly miss him. She was more concerned about how Elliot's death had changed them, their family. She was sure that was true. But this realization was something else she could never say.

When Meredith Wade stood to leave the den, she turned to Jillanna and said, "Want to walk me out?"

Jillanna nodded and followed, wanting to be near the woman who understood her.

Outside, Meredith Wade turned to her and said, "You understand that it wasn't your fault. You do understand that, don't you?" The woman seemed to need Jillanna to believe her. "You're just a child," she said.

Jillanna nodded. She felt a mouse-like curl in her throat. She bent her head and swallowed. Meredith Wade placed two palms on the top of Jillanna's head, lightly, as if forming a cap made of feathers. "Help your mother, Jilly. She needs you." Then the touch was gone.

Jilly. Only her closest friends called her Jilly, not grown-ups. As she watched Meredith Wade drive away in a VW Beetle the color of the sky, Jillanna wondered how the woman could know her so well. It was as if Meredith Wade could see into her heart like an angel.

The sun floated down through the branches of the sugar maples that lined the street and contentment slipped around Jillanna's shoulders. The heat of August rose from the sidewalk to caress her bare legs. She would have liked to spend the day at Carla's house out on the edge of town at the foot of the mountain. Carla's house was in the woods. The air was cool up there. They could play in the brook. But she knew that Meredith Wade was right; her mother needed her.

When she returned to the ladies and her mother on the couch, the room seemed brighter. When one by one, the visitors left, Jillanna hardly noticed. She was thinking about the way Meredith Wade's palms had cupped the top of her head, fleetingly, almost as if it hadn't happened, when her mother turned—one quick motion—and slapped Jillanna across the face with a flat hand.

Jillanna's cheek stung. She realized that they were the only two in the room.

Her mother said, "Don't you *ever* shout out like that again when grown-ups are talking. *Ever!*" She pushed the words out between her teeth. "Do you hear me?"

Jillanna's surprise overrode any tears. She nodded. She had never been hit in her life, had only seen slapping on television. She looked down and saw how her mother twisted her hands on her lap.

"How could you embarrass me like that on top of everything else?" her mother asked. "As if I had actually blamed you in private."

Then, Jillanna knew. Her mother *had* blamed her in private. If she had not distracted the lifeguard for attention that she didn't really need, Elliot might have been rescued. Did her father think that, too? She didn't know. She barely saw him. He worked more and more, sometimes into the night.

Her mother left the room without apology, shutting the door as if to close off the entire incident. Jillanna felt perfectly calm. Elliot's death was not her fault. She had Meredith Wade on her side: the kind words, the understanding words, and that floating touch on her hair to carry her through the day.

Jillanna didn't know if she was meant to stay in the living room or if she was free to leave. But go where? To her room? The kitchen? The house was as airless and as dark as a church.

She scooted to the edge of the couch and straightened her spine the way she had seen Meredith Wade sit on the edge of her chair. She attempted the graceful pose of Meredith Wade's hands folded still on her lap.

"You mustn't worry, Evelyn," she said in her fake grown-up voice to her mother, pretending she still sat in the room. "Your behavior is completely understandable. It's due to the shock and the grief." Her face flushed. What if her mother was listening on the other side of the door?

The backs of Jillanna's thighs felt hot and itchy on the rough couch and she thought again about her friends at the pool. No one had forbidden her from going back there.

These last couple of weeks her mother mostly ignored her as if she were a pet cat, expected only to appear now and then. Jillanna's father was too busy helping other people with their problems. Perhaps her parents thought that she wouldn't want to return to the scene of the accident, but she did. She did want to go back to the pool. She did.

She decided to leave the door of the den closed, as her mother had left it. She pushed Meredith Wade's chair aside and slipped out the window. She pressed her face through the foliage of the prickly hedge in front of their house. All clear. She raced across the sunburned lawn to the sidewalk. Walking seven blocks to the recreation center, she felt as if it were the first day of school vacation instead of nearing the last.

When Jillanna reached the main gate, she was surprised to find it latched. A sign read, "Closed for Repairs." Jillanna thought it strange that no repairmen worked or lingered. They must be away at lunch. The gate swung inward with a slight push, pulling Jillanna inside its fence of protection.

The swimming pool stretched out blue and sleek. Cicadas squealed raspy songs from the trees. Crickets chirped secretly in the grass. Mourning doves cooed from inside the shrubs. Jillanna imagined they were all trying to tell her that she was welcome here. She had never noticed these sounds before. For her, the swimming pool at the park had not been about peace and quiet, but friends wearing out voices that had been muted in school all winter. There was nothing like being in the center of the pack: the shouting, the confusion, the endless games of chase where you fought to be noticed, to be part of something, just enough to matter, but not enough to be "it."

So where was everyone since the pool was closed? Did they go to the mall without her? In the weeks past, Jillanna thought it was strange that none of her friends had called or come to see her after the funeral, although plenty of their mothers had passed along messages using words their kids would never say.

Now, with the insects and birds, Jillanna found that she didn't mind being there alone. The hot sun shone on the flat surface of the pool. She had always wanted to be the first to cannonball and break the transparent gloss of water, but children had rules and routines, like adults; they played "1-2-3 shoot" right up to the edge. The older kids never let Jillanna win. Today was her day.

Under her denim shorts and sleeveless blouse, Jillanna's white cotton camisole and underpants were damp with sweat. Her skin itched where her clothing had sharp tags at her neck and the back of her waist. The water looked cool. Jillanna dropped her shorts and shirt to the concrete.

As she approached the rim of the pool, she saw a mass of putty gray bobbing on the surface near the basket filter. It was a dead frog. Its arms and legs, spattered with black spots, created the shape of the letter X. Three limp dragonfly frames also floated, brushing up against the underbelly. Jillanna felt sick. The tea she had sipped all morning roiled in her gut and burbled into the sting which now clung to the back of her throat.

The clock from Town Hall two blocks away struck one. The repairmen might return soon. She had the chance, now, to plunge into the deep end and feel the weight of water on her skin press against her chest and thighs as she held her breath and counted up to twenty-seven Mississippi when she knew she would need to surface and replenish her pounding lungs. She imagined how her hair would spread like jellyfish tentacles and how her waist-high panties would buckle and fold against her bellybutton, an outie, just like Elliot's.

Elliot. How afraid he must have felt as he waved his tiny white arms and struggled against layer after layer of unrelenting water. Had he hit his head on someone's elbow—Billy's, Addie's, or Carla's—and been knocked instantly unconscious? Had they all swum over his dead body like feeder goldfish at the pet store? Jillanna began to imagine that instead of worrying about her raw fingers, she had taken Elliot to the baby pool to play with his boats. But it was too late for wishes. She faced the pool, wanting to feel the pressure of the water against her limbs, wanting to push all of the water away.

She loosened her hair from its ponytail, closed her eyes, and dove over the insect detritus and bloated frog.

She dove again and again, each time extending the length of her time underwater: twenty-eight, twenty-nine, thirty, and then finally stopping at thirty-five. Thirty-five Mississippi, a new record, just wait until she showed her friends.

She swam to the edge and held the top of her body out of the water to rest. Maybe one day, she would count underwater to thirty-five Mississippi in front of Meredith Wade, or maybe it would be her mother, who would place one hand softly on Jillanna's cheek, smile down at her as Jillanna gripped the side of the pool. Her mother would say, "Jilly, that was amazing."

The Third Element

Like a kid, Meredith counts down the final days of summer vacation. Twelve. Less than two weeks before the teacher in-service bullshit begins at the high school, and now this kid is skulking around her back porch threatening to waste her time.

She spies on him, a teenager, through the window of her studio in the back corner of the yard. A wrinkled undershirt and army-green shorts caked with dried mud drape his lanky frame as if he just woke up in a ditch. He's without shoes. She watches him cup his hands around his eyes and peer through the screen door into her kitchen.

If she holds completely still, he may not sense her presence, perched on the edge of her stool, leaning forward to hold back the curtain. She knows how to become motionless from the tedious hours of modeling for life drawing classes in college. Breathe into the pose and imagine the body suspended in space. He's probably harmless and will give up and go away.

When the guy raps on the screen door, Meredith lets the fabric slide out from between her fingers and leans back, heart jogging, though she can still see through the two-inch gap. She's reminded of a time when she played

Kick-the-Can in this yard with her neighborhood pack. She crouched next to this same shed, unobserved in the dark a few feet away from whoever was guarding the jail, thrilled with secrecy, but more, struck by an amplified sense of isolation while in such close proximity to another person. Watching him in secret reminds her of the time she first understood the pull of solitude. She shifts on her stool.

When he turns and looks out over the yard, she recognizes him, Sky, one of her seniors from last semester. She tries to remember something that stood out about him in class, or a clue as to why he'd show up on her porch, but she hasn't thought about students for weeks, especially not the ones from art history, a class she teaches with the lights out and slide images flashing on a screen. He was probably one of the last-minute seniors who required credits to graduate. She tends to remember how a student works with line and color, or a compelling piece, more than she remembers the personal interactions.

Now he sprawls on the wicker loveseat where Meredith likes to sip gunpowder tea at dawn, where her mother used to savor wine in the evenings. He folds his arms like an over-sized stick insect on a flake of bark, hands over his heart, a giant praying mantis boy. He closes his eyes. What does he want?

Meredith generally shrugs off small town curiosity, something she's always hated about living here. She holes up with her assemblage projects for weeks at a time. She can go days without speaking. The end of August marks a year since her mother's death. Meredith shuts herself away with an aim to channel loss and confusion into something tangible. Her table holds piles of sketches, diagrams of ideas for a series of framed collages, but the images remain flat before her. She has nothing more to show for nearly three months in the studio. Now Sky's settled in on her porch and seems to have fallen asleep.

She observes how his legs mimic the top branches of the birch in her yard, knobby and angular, like they'd be surprisingly strong under duress. She lifts a pencil from a jar and sketches the lines of his body on the newsprint covering her table. She hasn't drawn from a live figure since college. She certainly hasn't wanted to think about bodies since she watched her mother's waste away, a sheath of bones.

When she should get up and walk to the house to speak to him, she can't stop her wrist from flicking marks on the paper. The scratch of graphite and the trill of a wren in the garden, the disparate quality of two sounds, fill the distance between her and the boy, her hand jerking a pencil, his torso as calm as the August afternoon.

He raises an elbow to discourage a fly. She lifts her pencil, as if ceasing her strokes might still him. Drawing him feels like summer should, no stress, no thick dull strain of grief inside her chest.

Meredith hears her neighbor open the bedroom window and flap a sheet into the air, snapping it, three times. This practical motion brings Meredith to her senses. There is no real privacy in this town. There was more in Philadelphia where she went to art school. She looks at her drawing, black lines and gray—a form taking shape. It comforts her as drawings do.

When Sky stands, arches his back, and straightens, Meredith freezes. He knocks again on the flimsy wood of the screen door. She's reached a choice point. Of course, he would have seen her car in the driveway and suspect that she is home. He backs down the stairs to the lawn while looking up at the house. His movements are deliberate, as if he is easy in all things. She wants him to stay. She slides her pencil behind one ear and steps out of the studio and into the patch of sunlight near the climbing yellow roses on the fence.

"Hello," she calls, her throat filmy from not speaking all day. "I'm back here." She runs her fingers along the creamy petals of an open blossom, waiting for him to join her in the garden between the two buildings, wanting to watch him move.

"Hey, Ms. Webb." He stuffs his hands in his pockets, elbows branching out like a tire jack. His arms are freckled with splattered mud.

Meredith rubs her eyes to stop herself from staring at his arms, how they triangulate the space around him. "You graduated. You can call me Meredith. How are you, Sky?"

"I'm good. Yeah. I stopped by about the ad in the paper, the one about painting the house."

"What paper?" she says. She hasn't placed an ad, though she's aware that the house was scraped in preparation for fresh paint, a year ago last spring, before her mother needed hospice care. Meredith meant to see about it.

Sky unfolds a crumpled, brown-stained paper pulled from his pocket. "I found this in the barn."

She takes it from him and gets a whiff of horse sweat. *Wanted: House painter for small cape in town. Call Jolene Webb.* Her mother's phone number is listed, too.

A cool brush of air smelling of earthworms tickles the hair on Meredith's forearms and neck. She felt the visceral pulse of her mother's disembodied presence once before, the day after the memorial service, when Meredith listened to saved voice messages her mother had left her on her cell phone. That night, Meredith felt as if someone was walking around the house in sheepskin slippers on the pine floorboards. In the morning, she erased the messages.

Sky pulls on a branch from the rose trellis and says, "You've got some dead wood in here. Climbers need a hard pruning every fall. You could lose it all to disease."

Lose it all to disease. Meredith places her hand on her chest, clears her throat, nods. "I guess I need to think about getting a few things done around here."

Sky lets the branch spring back releasing a whiff of high summer scent. "I could fix this mess. Prune stuff *and* paint." He gestures to the paper in Meredith's fist. "I noticed the job hasn't been done. I'm looking for work away from the farm. I'm tired of all the horseshit, so to speak."

Meredith remembers how she felt when she wanted to get away and she wants to tell this boy to treasure his father, his home, the love he knows, but she knows he has to figure it out the hard way. She stuffs the ad into her pocket and rolls the tension from her shoulders. School starts for teachers in twelve days. She doesn't have time to paint a whole house or prune an arbor. She watches a wren dart past with a winged insect stuffed in his beak. The bird disappears into the wooden house hanging crooked on a nail in the fence. Meredith doesn't want to take care of houses and plants. She only sowed the vegetable garden in honor of her mother.

"How much do you charge?" she asks him.

"Twelve to fifteen an hour, depending on what I do."

"Let me think about it." She squints up at him. He's at least a foot taller than her. If he came by, she could continue to draw him, garner energy for her stalled project. "Stop by at nine tomorrow morning and we'll firm things up." Thinking about how she plans to study him, she hopes to sound strong and in charge, like she has clear boundaries.

"Sounds good." He nods.

Meredith watches him stroll away, slack jointed and light, down the alley between her house and garage. She pulls the scrap of paper from her pocket. The ad. She feels the cold again, as if her mother's exhale in death is prickling her skin.

"Okay, Mom, I get it," she says to the air around her. It feels good to stand in the middle of the yard and snap at her mother. "We'll paint the damn house."

Meredith arranges to have Sky start work in the garden. She draws him in secret as he bends to weed and stretches to prune. She moves from pencil and newsprint to velum and charcoal, but is careful to keep his features opaque. The sketches could be of any thin body.

She is awed by the strength coiled in Sky's weedy legs, like the copper cord she sometimes uses in her sculptures. At the end of the day when the two of them talk about the work he has done, she longs to wrap her hand around his wrist to see if she can meet thumb with finger, like she could her mother's wrist during the final days. In sickness, her mother had become sylphlike, but her slimming made her mother frail, while this boy's slender lines, taut and springy, seemed to snap the air like an electrical current.

She draws him for four more days. More paper piles on Meredith's table. She feels her mother watching over her shoulder, not as a spirit per se, but as a lingering consciousness of how they had both been changed by illness, gentler in their judgments of each other, softer in their interactions.

With only six days left until in-service, Meredith spends her evenings in the art room at school, sweeping remnants of spring projects and lining up new supplies on shelves. As she walks home, she notices that the dark air smells of apple cider and tomatoes, stagnant ditches and forest molds. She brings home copper wire and polymer clay. The pressure of diminishing time urges her to work late in her studio, turning sketches of Sky into figures that reach and fold like ballet dancers.

Now that her project is in full swing, she feels as if she could live on one pot of tea all day, but Sky brings her cucumbers and beans from the garden, and she eats these raw with late blueberries from the hedge.

The first time the boy stopped by the studio, she followed his eyes as they surveyed the room and glanced at the sketches. She couldn't tell if he recognized the forms as his own on the paper. She wasn't sure how she would explain it.

She felt relieved when he asked, "What was it like living in Philadelphia?"

"I lived in a studio apartment and worked in a café all morning so I could paint all afternoon and into the night. I was the volunteer curator for the café gallery in exchange for getting to show my work there once every summer when we were flush with tourists. I drank way too much coffee. I lived alone."

It felt strange to talk to a former student about her life away from Stark Run, not the part about painting, but the part about living alone.

"Do you like teaching?"

"Sure."

He picked up the top sheet from the pile of the figure sketches she had made earlier in the week and appeared to be reading the notes in the margins, measurements and letter codes about points and angles that only she could decipher. She bit a flap of skin from a thin blister on her index finger, nervous about his actual body, located so near to the wire figures, nervous he'd call her out.

"I really liked your class," he said. "I wish I hadn't waited until senior year to do the art thing." He set the drawing down. "I'm thinking about taking classes this fall."

She watched him cuff the edges of the pile until they were lined up. She admired his grace in the cramped quarters. She didn't know what to do with her hands. "That's great," she said. "They have a really good teacher on staff at the community college, a retired professor from The New England Institute of Art." She was pleased. He seemed to have natural aesthetic sensibilities.

He stretched his arm in a gesture that swept the space above the pile of jumbled wire forms. "All of this looks super cool."

He didn't seem to realize they were miniatures of him, but still, Meredith felt odd to have him probing her design process. Her work hadn't always been so private, but now it came out of loss, a study of how one lives in a body and then leaves a body. The idea of being seen from that dark place made her feel vulnerable.

"I only have a little bit more time before school starts. I should get back to work," she said.

He looked surprised, but nodded. She wanted to touch his arm to soften the brush-off; she turned to her worktable instead. Now Meredith keeps the drawings in the file cabinet, and when Sky drops off the snacks from the garden, he doesn't cross the threshold.

The house, gray with scraping, used to be flaky white. With two days left of summer vacation, Meredith tells Sky to leave the garden and start painting. She chooses daffodil yellow for the clapboards and a deep nasturtium shade for the trim. As Meredith stirs the paint, she says, "My mother's favorite color was yellow. She used to say it was the color of good health when she feng-shuied the living room. Well, good health to the whole neighborhood." She waves a wooden stirrer, twirling tiny circles like it's a magic wand. The paint fumes make her feel a little heady, reminiscent of sleepovers when half a dozen girls painted their nails in the attic room with the windows closed. "The door will be cerulean, the color of today's sky, Sky." She laughs at her own joke. "Did you hear a lot of sky jokes growing up?"

"A few," he answers, smiling.

But she's noticed that he doesn't make small talk anymore. He works hard and takes short breaks. She has him start painting on the rear side of the house where she can watch him from her studio. She sits at her worktable as he climbs the aluminum ladder and spreads paint across boards like butter on autumn corn. She put a hold on painting when she left Philadelphia to take care of her mother, but she remembers the pleasure she felt when paint left the brush and contacted the canvas, as if recording her gesture on linen meant keeping a part of herself that she also gave away.

Her hands rest quietly on her lap. She draws Sky with her eyes, sees ladder rungs through his clothes, hash marks across his body, like she'd been taught to draw people in school. He strokes on butter yellow; he is unaware.

The paint reminds her of ice cream. She must be hungry. She used to love ice cream until the day in the hospital, the day her mother died. Meredith ate ice cream directly from a cardboard carton while her mother watched from her bed. It's what her mother had asked her to do. She told Meredith not to worry so much about what she ate, that it didn't matter in the end, and to eat ice cream every day if she wanted. She told Meredith she would enjoy watching her only child eat ice cream as she left the world, as much as if she were eating it herself.

Meredith hasn't been able to stomach ice cream since. She realizes it's funny about mothers and daughters and love and hate. It had been just the two of them from the beginning. Day in and out, eating, talking, and moving into their separate rooms in the evenings to pursue their independent solitude, which increased with the years. As a teenager, she could hardly stand to be near her mother for more than a few hours, but now an absence fills her chest cavity in spurts, like buckshot, leaving tiny spaces for hot and cold to seep in and send her into hiding.

Meredith hears Sky singing the song rapping in his ears from his iPod. When he's got the wall half-finished, Meredith walks to the store and buys caramel coffee ice cream. She wonders if eating ice cream with another person will help her move past the day in the hospital when her mother grabbed Meredith's hand and squeezed with the grip of a hawk. The monitor sounded the telltale steady beep for over a minute before Meredith felt her mother's fingers release. Meredith feels a part of her mother still holding on.

At the end of the day, while Sky cleans the brushes in the bucket with the hose, Meredith stands on the back porch with two bowls. "Hey, Sky. Want some ice cream?"

"Sure. Let me just finish here."

Meredith sets his bowl on the steps and sits in the love seat. The ice cream slides along the base of her throat, tasting like the smell of exterior enamel, like toxic yellow, like the hospital room. She dumps the rest of her portion into the flowerbed.

"Hey, whoa," Sky says and laughs as he walks over, shaking water out of the brushes. "Why'd you do that?"

"It's not my flavor. It smells like paint."

He sits down on the steps and takes a spoonful of his ice cream. The male wren warbles from the rosebush in the corner of the yard.

"It's mind over matter," he says with the spoon in his mouth. "I did a social studies report on this theory." He turns to face her. "It's called Vedic consciousness." He balances the bowl on his palm. He stretches out the other with the spoon, both arms fully extended. He stands and walks to the lawn to wobble across a hose in the grass as if walking a tightrope. "I tell myself I can stay on this hose, and I do."

Meredith hasn't heard Sky speak this many words in a week or do anything silly in fun. She decides to play along. "Careful not to fall," she says.

The color of the landscape around him seems amplified, as if the bushes and flowers are alerted to attention like Meredith is by his motion.

"I've been practicing the concept that thoughts and words hold power in manipulating my surroundings. It works." He reaches the sprinkler at the end of the hose, steps off, and returns to the porch. "There's a belief that consciousness is more than mere brain activity, but a separate entity, an energy apart from the body that the brain can manipulate with thought, and so forth. Here, take my bowl. Hold it to your nose and close your eyes. Smell the ice cream and think ice cream. Coffee ice cream."

Meredith accepts. The smell of coffee, extra sweet in the melting, presents her with an image of a shared studio space in Philadelphia, where she thrived on caffeine and paint fumes. She needed long stretches of solitude to work and lost the desire for sleep, and friends, and home. Only her mother's illness could bring her back to Stark Run. She wished she'd found the courage to draw her mother, but illness had not eased her mother's excessive need for privacy.

Sky asks, "What do you smell now?"

"Philadelphia," she says.

"Wow. Okay, well, that's weird. That's something else, then." He hands her his spoon. "Take a bite."

She stares into the bowl and studies the tawny moat surrounding a small hill as if she is reading tea leaves and can see her future. Using his spoon, eating from his bowl, seems to cross a boundary. What is she thinking? The paint fumes make her dizzy.

"There's more to it. I don't think I can." She thrusts the bowl at him. "You finish it. I really bought it for you."

He shrugs. He takes the bowl and bends to eat, hunching his knobby shoulders into a curve. Meredith is grateful that his body is turned and he cannot see her watching him, staring at his scapula, and the bone of his hip. Her fingers itch for clay. She leans back in her seat. "Tell me about the classes you're taking this fall."

The next morning, Meredith drags three empty wooden canvas stretchers the size of rock star posters from the garage into a rectangle of hot sunlight on the driveway. She wipes off the dust and cobwebs with the hem of her skirt.

Last night after the ice cream, she told herself that she needed to stop stalking the kid. Today, Sky works on the opposite side of the house, but she can hear him sing as she paints the frames with shiny black enamel for a triptych sculpture—maiden, mother, crown. The air feels dense. Time is slim. Her vision for the project seems dull, the themes overdone.

A reviewer once wrote . . . *Meredith Webb shapes three-dimensional pictorial statements using object displacement to represent absurdity in American culture.* Ridiculous, she thought, when she'd read it. She had no such thing in mind. When she works, she responds to an impulse to sand and paint and glue and wire. She found the review political and reaching. Reading it made her want to slam doors, the way she did as a teenager. She's lost heart, and now fears what a reviewer might say about repression and third-wave feminism if she shows a triptych about the evolution of woman.

While the stretchers dry against the wall of the garage, she flips off her shoes and sits in the grass on the front lawn to look at them. She leans back on her elbows. School starts tomorrow. Maybe it will be different, her second year. Maybe she'll try and reach out more to students—students like Sky—help them make connections between their natural impulses and their work.

When Meredith was ten, her mother moved the two of them to this house and Meredith began fourth grade in a new school. Her mother gave her art supplies: Bristol paper, beeswax crayons, and a set of ebony pencils. She told her that it can be hard to adjust to a new place, and she could use the paper to draw about her feelings. Meredith used up a whole pad making black circles and filling them with grainy color. When she ran out of paper, her mother gave her more.

When Meredith cleaned out a hall closet last winter, she found seven sketchpads filled with pages and pages of circles and spirals, brought alive with soft strokes of crayon. Her mother had dated them as if they were journals. Meredith sat on the floor, pressed against boots, and looked through every one.

Now as she gazes at the frames against the garage, she can't stop thinking of possibilities for filling the space within them. She likes the shape they make, lined up in a row, black against the white backdrop. What they need is something inside the emptiness, but what?

She sits up and squints. She rubs the grass imprints on the skin above her elbows with the tips of her fingers, her arms cradled, holding herself. An idea flits in, like a phantom wren, shy, as if she has caressed it into courage. Her assemblages are not about culture or merely an impulse to use her hands. She realizes that what she wants to do is illuminate space inside form with some third element. Where line becomes shape is entirely dependent on the area that surrounds it and dwells within it.

It was Sky, that afternoon when he first showed up, who taught her this, the way his clothes dangled on his bones like loose skin, like the skin of a dying mother. That's what compelled Meredith to shape the lines of his figure, as if documenting a body could keep it alive.

She approaches the frames as if they are relics. One by one, she hauls each one from the garage to her studio. She works quickly to bolt them together in a row and props them against her bookshelves. She pauses and kneels before them. As sunlight moves across the yard and the natural light inside her studio fades to a dusky pink, the air turns cool. Her mother's presence has entered the room. She weeps. She hears the boy outside take down his ladder, hose off his brushes. His truck pulls away from the street out front with a racket that makes her smile. She relaxes.

At her table, she studies the sketches, then fashions steel wire ladders within the space of the three frames at odd levels. With more wire, she adheres the copper and clay figures to and from the ladders, creating a circus of lithe floating forms. The figures are suspended in place and time, miniature effigies, replicating a woman's body before disease took the whole thing.

Bench Girls

The three teenage girls perched on top of the park bench shouldn't have been there, their stinking cigarettes, their foul-faced glances. What about school? This was Jack's special time, his after play-school fresh-air time with his granddaughter.

"Higher, Pop-Pop," Mandy May cried from her swing.

"You got it," Jack said, though his heart wasn't in it.

He had seen these girls before, taking up most of the sidewalk in front of the hardware store. They shoved each other into boys who mooned around them, boys who slouched, standing as if height had invaded their unsuspecting bodies and they didn't feel right in their clothes, their laughter high-strung and unnatural. Jack had been a boy like that. He remembered how the girls he could push down in a game of tag transformed into something altogether terrifying. It happened overnight. You went to bed a lord and woke up a servant. And here they were, a version of those girls from his younger days, only these three with their piercings, dark eyeliner, and scruffy get-ups looked as though they'd been put through the wringer.

One option was to take Mandy May to play up at the farm. He'd grown up there without a fancy playground, but Mandy May loved the swings down here. His wife would say the girls were harmless. They were just making a statement; all kids do it. Molly knew what was what in the world. She knew how to remain calm, tolerate others, but now she was gone. For three months! An internship at a yoga center! He'd quit the hardware store to spend more time with her and she left. She was as gone as a person can get outside of death as far as he was concerned, at least for a little while. Then she'd come home. If she were here now, she would tell him to relax.

He loosened his jaw, making circles with his chin—three times clockwise, three times counterclockwise, the way Molly had taught him, followed by deep breaths. They're just girls. They'll leave. He ground his right foot forward in the gravel. leaned, and pushed Mandy May higher.

"Good one, Pop-Pop!"

"Just showing you my best stuff, little missy."

Molly's philosophy was to focus on the positive, look around for beauty, trust the natural order of things. There'd been cold rain and winds for most of September. The last Sunday in September brought a hard frost on the farm, late for Vermont. But now an Indian summer sun streamed mid-day heat through half-naked branches. It was a gift. It made everyone a little giddy. The park smelled of leaf rot, the scent of changing seasons, Jack's favorite. The light, the leaves gold and burnt orange on the trees, even the tidy buildings lined up on the street repeating themselves seemed gorgeous. But the girls were like pigeons sitting there, an imported species. They ruined the splendor. Jack scowled and pushed Mandy May higher.

"Wheee," she cried.

From the bench a laugh came from the girl on the left, the one with the honey-colored hair. He watched the girl lean forward, hovering over the other two. They were hunched over a cell phone. Except for the combat boots with the pink shorts and a few chains dangling from her hip, she looked the most normal of the three.

Her hair swept like sunlight across bare shoulders. Bangs framed her face. The look of her and the smell of cigarettes reminded Jack of Molly at that age, the alto he'd fallen for during a choir weekend in the mountains, senior year in high school, about a thousand years ago; she was new in town. He'd first seen her with a group of girls smoking behind the shower house and was knocked flat by her beauty, but more, he could tell by the way the other girls looked at her that she held the power. Her laugh was rich, while the other girls seem to cackle. She was the real deal.

He couldn't remember exactly what Molly looked like back then, her features, the details, he meant, up close. Could he remember what she looked like now? She'd only been gone a couple of weeks. A slight panic consumed him. He tried to picture Molly in yoga pants in a pose like the gray-haired ladies in the catalog she had left on the end table by her comfy chair. He admitted the women at the yoga center did look healthy for their age, their bodies fit, and their skin taut and glowing. He searched his mind to find Molly's face on a yoga body. There it was; he found it, and felt relieved.

Mandy May whomp-wobbled the swing from left to right. "Where's your head, Jack?" Mandy May—asked, something Molly would ask and not necessarily expect an answer.

Heat rose up his neck to his face. He felt they had all been reading his mind, Mandy May and those girls, which was ridiculous, of course, but there was never any doubt when old Jack felt embarrassed, all rashy-pink, right there for the world to see it. Then he remembered that he was the grown-up here. He stood taller and rolled his shoulders back.

"Never you mind what's in my head. The important thing is what's in yours," he said. Focus, Jack, he told himself. She was a character, that Mandy May, pretending to be Molly, a little monkey-see, monkey-do. "Just pump your legs like I showed you."

"Dah, dah, dah," she sang and pumped.

"That's it. Now you're doing it."

He glanced back at the girls on the bench chattering like three sets of those trick teeth they sold at the hardware store at Halloween. The girl in the middle was the ringleader. Clearly. Her hair stuck out from beneath a ratty baseball cap in thatches, chopped-up lengths, orange, green, and bleached-out white. Her over-sized pants and shirt looked as if she had rummaged a brother's dirty laundry basket. Molly would say she was the kind of girl who took care to look as though she could care less and that this was what gave her power. The girl passed a brown cigarette that smelled like cloves. Mandy May should not have to see people polluting their lungs like that; she was five for Christ sake. The girl looked at Jack, arching one eyebrow, daring him to look away.

"Come on, Pop-Pop, higher."

"Hold on tight," he said, an excuse to break eye contact. After one last ride, they would leave and head up the hill to the farm where Mandy May would be safe. "We're going to let it fly this time."

Mandy May squealed. He glanced back at the girls. The teenager in the middle took twice as many drags as she passed the cigarette back and forth to the other two. Yep. The ringleader. Molly would be right, as usual.

All of his life Jack had come across bad-mannered women among the good, and still did. Earlier that week, the receptionist at the dentist office barely looked up from her computer when he stepped into the waiting room, even though the placard had spelled it out: Announce Your Arrival. The cashier at the grocery store tossed a can of beans on top of his bananas. The redheaded librarian who smelled like garlic and coffee snapped her fingers in the direction where he might look for a book instead of getting off her butt to help him. He could find his own book, but still, what happened to basic manners? The girls on that bench at the park were bound to become like those women if they weren't careful. Women like that made people feel invisible, like thin air.

Molly had way more substance than that. She treated him like a king, which made her a queen. If he had appreciated her more, perhaps he would not be spending the cool autumn nights alone while she slept in a dorm. But Molly had said that her journey had nothing to do with him, which was supposed to make him feel better. It made him feel worse. When did she start saying things like *her journey*? And how could *her journey* have nothing to do with him? They were in this life together.

She'd been gone three weeks, seven more weeks to go. Every day, he felt more restless. That day, the bench girls distracted him from that lonely feeling, if only for a little while. He wondered if he would see them next time at the park. He hoped he would, and then as soon as he thought that, he felt ashamed. He couldn't figure out why he would want to expose Mandy May to their behavior, or why he would want to submit himself to the discomfort he felt around them, yet he found himself thinking about them too much. He wondered what they were like in class and at home. Did they have boyfriends? When he thought about their bodies, particularly the honey-blond in tight clothes, he scolded himself. What kind of pervert was he? It was insane the way thoughts about those girls filled the emptiness he felt with Molly gone.

He needed a project, but the garden was nearly put to rest and the barn was tidy. He could drive up to see his fishing buddy in the Northeast Kingdom, but now he watched Mandy May two days a week, so there was that.

He'd just have to think of ways to make his time with Mandy May fill him up. Maybe he could watch her a third day. Maybe he should go back to the hardware store, but part-time. He laughed. Last fall, he couldn't wait to retire, go hiking with Molly, and watch her bake at the kitchen counter while he listened to talk radio. They were going to work on their sex life. Now he was thinking about getting a job, all because Molly had left him here alone, all because of those girls.

Get a grip, Jack, he told himself. Get a goddamn fucking grip. With no chores or appointments and no Mandy May today, the afternoon stretched before him, long and hollow. He had a new book from the library. He had a bruised banana. He took both out to the yard and stretched on the cedar chaise lounge that their youngest had built in woodworking class his senior year. Crazy Sky, who lived a few miles away from home, couch surfing at a friend's house, just to get away from his old man. Everybody seemed to be looking for some space away from Jack. He missed his kids. He missed Molly. Now he felt too tired to read. He fell asleep.

The next day, Jack picked up Mandy May at noon from school. He couldn't remember an autumn so much like summer and he'd lived in Stark Run his whole life. The sky was clear and wide, the air clean coming down off the mountains. Leaves blew and collected in the drained swimming pool behind the rec center. It was dance class day. Normally Molly took her to that. Mandy May loved wearing her tutu and he was not to forget it and he didn't. But the weather was too great to stay cooped up inside at the rec center.

"Hey, Mandy. How about we skip dancing? There won't be many days like this left to play outside without our coats. You can dance inside all winter."

"Sure, Pop-Pop." She twirled her tutu, the color of bubble gum. "We just won't mention it to Mom-Mom."

Jack's face flushed. What made Mandy May think of keeping a secret from Molly? Jack knew he should address the slip into gray area. But if he brought it to light, he'd have to do the right thing, take her to dance class in a stuffy gym on a glorious afternoon. Maybe miss the next episode of the bench girls. By the time Molly got home, Mandy May will have forgotten all about skipping the class and the fact that they had a secret.

"I want to swing, Pop-Pop."

"Okay, we'll go to the park."

There. He neither agreed about keeping the secret from Molly, nor denied. Jack shook his head. He had been general manager of a large store for thirty-five years in a town where a hundred different people needed a hundred different things every week. What had happened to his life that these were the kind of conundrums—to dance or to swing—he now faced?

When Jack and Mandy May arrived at the swing set, and saw the empty bench, he felt disappointment wave through him. Of course, the girls couldn't skip school to suit his schedule. He reminded himself he was there for the fresh air and he used all his mental might to soak up autumn, smell the mushrooms, and listen for the geese. Mandy May decided to ride the dinosaur teeter-totter. She sang to the brachiosaurus. Jack leaned against a tree and watched her. He thought about the night before, when Molly called. She had cried and said she missed him.

"It's the auryvedic cooking. I'm de-toxing. It makes me weepy."

"Then come home, Moll. Come home."

"I can't. This is good for me. I have to do this." She ended the call. It was time for her meditation hour.

Jack had felt better that Molly felt sad and for a while he puttered around his shop in the barn feeling lifted. She was miserable without him. Then his mood spiraled down when he realized what an ass he was, how selfish. He'd spent the rest of the night in the living room reading about her program from the brochure. He read between the lines, trying to understand what she had allowed to kidnap her. Were they brainwashing her? He'd be sure to listen carefully to her on the next phone call. He skipped watching their favorite sit-com as a sign of solidarity since Molly's dorm didn't have television. For a long time, he sat in her chair with the lights off.

Now Jack sat on the park bench as Mandy May flung the tetherball around the post. He should stand up and teach her how to punch the ball, but he hadn't slept well and felt more tired than usual. He watched her do a cartwheel in the grass. She ran and hid. She tagged trees. "You're it."

He wished he could make friends with trees and believe they were sentient beings that could make him feel less lonesome, in the way that Mandy May could. He was beginning to feel like a failure at this, the simple task of nurturing a child.

More cartwheels. More tagging. He envied all of her energy, but it felt good to sit there when he was supposed to be somewhere else. He kicked the leaves piling up at the base of the bench, more and more leaves each day. When was the last time he had kicked a pile of dry leaves like a kid? Maybe he could learn how to relax, like Molly begged him to, just by watching Mandy May. Maybe the park was still a good place to come.

Jack did not see the girls for the rest of the week, but he continued to think about them, and the following Monday, they were back. How many days can a person hook school before they get caught? He didn't care, really; they were here, and their presence was no longer a threat, but an intrigue. The girls' presence gave him a lift. Jack watched them, a little less careful to hide his glances than the time before. Another glorious week of an Indian summer was predicted. The day was dry, bright and sunny. He felt young.

The blond girl badgered the ratty-looking girl. "Right, Reese. Don't you think so, Reese?"

She kept slipping off the edge of her perch, leaning, craning her neck. They should just sit on the bench the regular way and relax, Jack thought. If they were taking a day off, they should enjoy it.

The girl's shirt, purple and peach and sky blue like rainbow sherbet, clung to her shape. Jack's oldest, Trish, Mandy May's mother, had worn tight shirts at that age, too, and tie-dyed. It was what girls did, he supposed, and he'd appreciated it as a boy, but not so much as a father, in fact, not at all. Too much information was what Molly would have said. Mandy May wouldn't have to go in that direction. He could teach her. Keep a body healthy was all. Focus on the mind. Still Jack couldn't help but glance at the girl and admire her looks.

She gasped and panted as she spoke. "Did I show you the birthday bracelet my uncle sent from New York? You can borrow it, if you want to, Reese."

The air smelled musky, like burnt toast. What were they smoking this time? He couldn't hear everything that the girls said or stare at them too long without Reese catching him and smirking. It was important to Jack that they not think he was a dirty old man. He tried not to think of them as objects; Molly had trained him. His focus on the girls was more a study, he told himself. To help him help Mandy May prepare to grow up.

As Mandy May rose and fell from the sky on her swing, she chattered to a squirrel on a branch of the oak that shaded the swing set. Jack hoped she was thinking loftier thoughts than those bench girls. She smelled like kid sweat and waxy crayon. That's what he would focus on, the innocence of childhood, and what he could teach her.

"That's a gray squirrel, Mandy May. A *gray* squirrel. There are little red ones, too, in the rock wall up at the farm. They're different, less cheeky."

"Pop-Pop, where does the squirrel sleep when it's snowing?"

"Are you thinking about winter on this hot day?" She was so like Molly. The curiosity and compassion, how do you bottle that stuff up? "In a nest, I guess, a leafy nest. Way up high."

Mandy May looked up. He imagined the cogs and wheels churning, Mandy May grappling with the validity of his answer. Soon she wouldn't take everything he said as heaven's own truth. She'd become a skeptic, sullen, like the rest of them. But what were those bench girls saying now? He pushed the swing faster to keep Mandy May from talking.

"So, *do* you want a turn wearing the bracelet, Reese?" The girl ached and Jack ached right along with her. As a boy, he, too, had groped for approval. It was painful to re-live.

Reese puffed and passed the cigarette. She gazed, squinting, into the baseball field on the other side of the park, like someone was about to nab a fly ball and the sun was in her eyes, though Jack hoped she would catch his eye again. Something about the earlier look had made him feel less bored with the task of pushing a swing. Now it was as if she wouldn't look at him on purpose, like she knew he wanted her to.

The blond girl practically quivered, coiled for any sign of Reese's attention. He wasn't much different, cloying for acknowledgment. He watched her twirl the end of her hair.

Molly had been a hair twirler. The gesture had caught his eye at choir camp. He'd fantasized that if he could only be her hair, she could spin him around and around. Everything surrounding Molly had flitted and sparkled, her rope of followers in tow, bright and rounded, like the blond girl on the bench, not like the ratty girl, a black cloud. The difference was, back then, it was the girls like Molly, smart and on track, who wielded the power. When he was young, all the girls, power or not, had been soft and clean and golden.

"So, do you want it, Reese?"

"Shut the fuck up, Sharyn."

Whoa! He hadn't heard much from that other one, the third girl on the right, dragging out each syllable.

"Can you just shut-the-fuck-up?"

Jack pulled his expression into a glower as best he could. Reese looked at him and laughed. She slid down to sit on the bench properly. The blond girl copied her, then Sharyn.

Jack hadn't caught the other girl's name, but watch your language, missy, he thought. Potty-mouth, he'd call her. Potty-mouth was perfectly relaxed, or was she? She split the ends of her hair with Day-Glo orange-painted fingernails. Trish had had the same habit when she was a teen and it had driven him crazy, the fact that she struggled with something difficult, in secret, on the inside, him powerless. Molly had handled it directly, on her own, told her *cut it out, it's ruining your looks*, and went about her business. She didn't stew and ponder and question. She dealt out the truth, plain and simple.

"It's from New York. I thought you'd want to wear it."

Sharyn sat back a little and faced front. Glum is what he'd call that face, like she might cry. All three of the girls stopped talking.

"Three little kittens have lost their mittens . . ." Mandy May sang.

Reese held on to the cigarette and blew smoke out of her nose. Jack had never been able to do that when he tried to like smoking years ago.

". . . and they began to cry."

Reese dropped the butt into the leaves under the bench with her black boot.

"Pop-Pop, say, Meow! You forgot to say Meow!"

Jack said *Meow*, though he didn't want to with those girls sitting there. He hoped that his little granddaughter had not seen Reese litter the stub of the cigarette. Where was the citizenship? With his courage, that's where. He decided to speak.

"That cigarette could start a fire with everything so dry, with the leaves there, and all."

The girls didn't acknowledge him. Perhaps they thought he was speaking to Mandy May. He cleared his throat.

"Better check that cigarette in those dry leaves."

Reese glared at him.

"Whatever," said Potty-mouth. She kept her head bent down over her phone.

"Sorry, sir," said Sharyn. She crouched in the leaves, scattered them about and found the butt. She stamped it to bits with the heel of her boot. "Come on, Reese. We should go."

But Reese just continued staring at Jack, no expression now, just an empty face. Sharyn shoved her hands in the back pockets of her jeans and sat down on the very edge of the bench, ramrod straight, as if ready to flee at a given notice.

He was about to thank Sharyn, when a chevron of geese passed overhead, honking their farewells. Mandy May tipped back in her swing to watch.

"Three, four, five geese, Pop-Pop!"

That's right, Mandy May. Keep it light. Just like Molly. Bless them both. Yet he could not be sure how much of the brief interaction with the bench girls, the nuances, his granddaughter understood.

"Good, Mandy May. Five. Good counting."

Long curls brushed Jack's cheek as he leaned to cup the edges of the vinyl seat with his palms. Mandy May smelled of the golden shampoo that Molly kept for her granddaughter in the guest bathroom back at the house. The tenderness he could feel for this child just by the smell of her. Focus on Mandy May.

Another week passed. Still no rain, still no Molly, but a cold front had moved in and snow flurries mixed with falling beech leaves. Jack zipped the hood of Mandy's jacket tightly around her face. Today would be one of the last days at the park until spring.

After he'd pushed Mandy May for a while, the girls arrived and approached the bench. He noticed his mouth had curled into a smile. When he realized it, he pulled it into a frown. The girls sat down and immediately huddled around their phones.

Focus, Jack told himself. He looked up at the sky. A crow flew high across the baseball field and landed in a tree. The creak of the swing's rusted hardware cut the crisp air in a harsh rhythm. It was a simple problem, one he could fix. Jack made a note to come down later in his truck with a ladder and some WD-40.

Smoke wafted from the bench to the swings. Jack figured out by now that their rolled cigarettes were mixed with pot and he wondered what led a person to use drugs. Statistics showed every day how easily confidence could fracture, suddenly, especially in girls. Queen Bee and wannabes, like in that book Molly read a few years back in her library group. Self-harm, pills, sex.

"Check this out." Potty-mouth waved her cell phone like a flag. "Destiny gave Ricky Billings a blowie in the art

room? Ms. Webb walked in and caught him there with his
pants down. She pitched a fit! Jizz all over public property."
She laughed.

Jack flushed. All of that, the pot, the language, and now
the smut right in front of a child and an old man. Potty-
mouth had some issues. He scowled but they were too far-
gone, practically hooting and rolling, to notice his glare.

"Ew, Claudia, that's so gross," said Sharyn, but her mouth
was wide with delight.

Gross indeed, Miss *Claudia* Potty-mouth. That's it,
Mandy May and he were moving. It was his job to protect
his grandchild. Molly would have a cow if she knew Jack
had allowed Mandy May to hear and see this behavior.

"How about some lunch, Mandy May?"

"I'm hungry, Pop-Pop," said Mandy May and whimpered. She slid her butt a smidge off the swing so her toes
could reach the depression of dirt beneath her. She scuffed
her shoes to slow herself. He could hear Molly's voice. *You
really shouldn't let her scuff up her shoes like that at the
swings, Jack. Kids' shoes cost an arm and a leg. They need
firm rules.* But didn't they also need to feel that they
controlled the speed of their own swings so they didn't
turn out grasping for acceptance from others like the
Sharyns of the world?

The swing jerked from left to right, twisting, until Mandy
May jumped off, and fell forward into the grass. She rolled
and lifted herself up.

"Ta-da!" he said in the way they all did whenever Mandy
May fell and got back up. At least, he remembered to do
that.

He felt proud of her smiling, sweaty, peach-glow face.
She was fresh and young and good. He looked over to see
if the girls saw her, too, and appreciated what a precious
child she was, as strangers sometimes did with children,
but the girls' heads were glommed together as if they were

sheep. Reese's thumbs twitched over the keys on the cell phone. The inside of his chest felt dull, in the way it felt when he took long walks across the frozen field on winter nights, arrived back to the house, and looked into the lit rooms, his family inside, feeling the loneliness of being on the outside of something warm. Jack steadied the swing with his hand, settled it back to stillness. Silly. Why would they care about an accomplished child when jizz splattered the art supplies? Get ahold of yourself, Jack. Mandy May ran to him. She grabbed the sleeve of his shirt and tugged.

"Come on, Pop-Pop."

"Let's go, girl."

She led him to the blanket under the tree where he had set their lunch box. Jack was happy for the distraction, Mandy's highs and lows, the liveliness of her. If she hadn't pulled him away, he would still be standing at the swings like a moron.

When his granddaughter opened her lunchbox, la-la-la-ing, Jack smelled peanut butter sandwich, sliced peaches, and chocolate mint cookies, the lunch Molly had told him to make, not very Aura Vedic from the little he knew about it. He sat down in the grass among the leaves, his back propped against the oak. He couldn't see the bench girls from here and he was grateful. They'd taken things too far. Jack thought that he and the girls could cohabitate the park and respect one another's space. He thought they could make life a little interesting, not complicated. Now he just felt tired. He needed about twenty years of sleep against this tree, and then Molly could come wake him and Mandy May, and take them home.

Like in the Rip Van Winkle story, by then, the whole world would have changed the game. People like Ratty Reese, and Potty-mouth Claudia, who underneath their façades were probably as frightened as lambs, would be called out for their behavior. The Sharyns would have a

Jodi Paloni

chance for the spotlight. The Mollys would shine. Humanity teetered and thrived in turn. Givers and takers. Queen bees and wannabes. Time would prove it once again. The thing was, by sleeping, maybe he could avoid the burden of caring but not being able to help.

Mandy May slipped into his lap. He remembered where he was and why. She lifted her fingers to his ear. She tugged his lobe and rolled it between her thumb and forefinger, oily with peanut butter. He felt Mandy May's form become limp with sleep. His chest lifted from the inside as he recognized this act of trust. He felt in that moment that perhaps he could save her, love her enough, cloak her. Molly would be home before he knew it. Four weeks down. Six to go. Simple math.

He watched Mandy May's wrist dangle at his hip, the crust of her sandwich clenched in a fist in a patch of dust where the grass had been worn. He felt his first real contentment of the afternoon. Teenage girls far enough away, the chatter rose and fell. Sound and pitch. Gossip and cigarettes. Texting and sexting. Relax. People did the downtown deed in backrooms in his day, *blowies*, as well. It wasn't a new invention, only a new name. Nothing ever really changes. There was just a hell of a lot more of it. Relax. Breathe.

The breeze picked up and tumbled leaves around Jack's body and he lay there enjoying the scent of it. He saw a woman walking across the baseball field. It was Molly! She walked past Jack. Molly! She sat on a swing and waved to the girls sitting on the bench. Tree branches undulated, rustling the few remaining leaves clinging to summer. Sharyn leapt from the bench and joined Molly. Their swings alternated the forward and back pattern, pumping higher. They laughed and the laughter echoed from the woods on the edge of the park. Molly reached out to grab Sharyn's hand. The swings wobbled and the girls giggled and the branches waved. Molly dragged her feet to pace her swing along with Sharyn's. They were in sync. Their honey-blond heads angled towards each other. More laughter. Claudia sat on the bench. Her voice robotic-like and hollow, "Shut the fuck up. Just shut the fuck up." Reese stood, glaring, and approached the swingset. She walked between Sharyn and Molly, breaking the chain of their hands. She scuffed her feet through the leaves and stood by the trunk of the picnic tree. She blocked his view from Molly.

This close, he saw the bones of her wrists under the cuff of her baggy shirt. They were bird bones. Reese poked the side of his ribs with the toe of her boot. A shock ran through his body.

"Hey, asshole, you left the little kid. What if I was some sick perv? What world do you live in?"

He lifted himself, propping up on his elbows, his torso still fixed to the ground.

Reese laughed. "Did ya lose someone?" Reese reached down and grabbed a baggie from the lunch box. She popped sandwich crusts into her mouth and made an exaggerated sound, imitating a monster eating a small animal.

He shook his head. "Mandy May?" He tried to move his leaden legs. "Mandy, girl!"

Mandy May stepped from behind the tree, laughing. "She's so funny, Pop-Pop." She looked up at Reese. "I like her hair."

Jack's heart slammed inside his ribs. Adrenaline surged, but he felt frozen to the ground. No, no, no you don't. You don't like her hair. He should stand. He wanted to grab Mandy May to his chest. He looked around for Molly. The swings were empty. He couldn't move. Reese's boot tips were pressed against the side of his hip, as if they could hold him there with the slightest pressure.

When Mandy May plopped into his lap and wrapped her arms around his chest, Reese stepped away. She dropped the empty sandwich bag, which floated down and landed on the bridge of his nose.

"Pop-Pop!" Mandy May giggled.

"Later, dudes," said Reese.

When she was gone, Jack shifted Mandy and lay back into the leaves, arms spread out, his body a T. He was shaken, the bag with peanut butter stuck to his face. Mandy May removed the bag. She wet her thumb with spittle and wiped the peanut butter from his nose, the way Molly would have cleaned Mandy May's face. He closed his eyes. It had taken a four-year-old to save him.

On the drive home from town, Jack thought of Molly, who had cut his hair for forty years, kept laying hens and meat birds to build a college fund for all five kids, as if she hadn't done enough keeping the household and the homework afloat, the teenage meltdowns and minor traffic infractions all cleaned up, and who didn't deserve to have to contend with his slip ups with Mandy May. He wondered if he should call Molly and tell her what happened, but nothing really happened. An impending scolding loomed with the dark clouds, and the cold front that was moving in.

Now, in the warmth of the farmhouse, with Mandy May here, chattering to the people in the pictures of women in Molly's catalog, a little squirrel in her grandmother's comfy chair, he fell in love with his wife all over again, as he did from time to time when she was gone and he missed her. He didn't need to tell her. She'd just worry he couldn't keep a close enough watch and the time at the yoga center was for her to focus on herself. He bent over Mandy May's shoulder.

"I thought we'd go to Ice Cream Castle on the way to meet your mom for one last taste of summer."

"Yippee!"

"Hop in the truck. And on my way back home, Mandy May, I'm going to stop at the park and fix the creaky swing."

"That's a good choice, Pop-Pop."

He lifted her out of the chair and folded her into a hug. She leaned back and patted his cheeks.

In the middle of the night, the telephone jarred Jack out of a deep sleep.

"Hello."

"Jack."

"Molly, is that you?"

There was crying on the other end of the line. Jack rubbed his head with his free hand until he felt awake.

"What is it, Moll?"

"I'm homesick."

Jack laughed. "It's the middle of the night."

"I'm sorry. I tried to meditate. I was starving."

"What do you mean?"

"We can only eat what we can fit inside a bowl. It's a monk thing. We get this bowl and we fill it and that's all we get. Usually I'm all right, but tonight I felt like ordering a pizza. I'm in the parking lot. I've sprung myself!"

"Molly!"

"I know. I met the delivery boy out here in my pajamas and now I'm sitting in the car and I've eaten half of it. I automatically saved the other half for you. And then I missed you and so I called. I couldn't stop thinking about you." She laughed, a soft sound in the cold night.

Jack felt his heart pump faster and his torso flush with goose bumps. After choir camp, they'd become inseparable, as much as possible, but their parents wouldn't let them go out on school nights so they used to talk on the phone until they fell asleep. Right after graduation they were married. They went to community college and lived in a cabin on the brook on the far edge of the hayfield. They made their way through school, but they were so wrapped up in the exploration of each other's bodies not much else mattered. Thinking about those times and his wife in the dark car breaking a rule a hundred miles away aroused him. He turned onto his back, and shifted himself inside his pajamas, resting his free hand on his erection.

"Jack, I broke my promise to the program, but what bothers me is that I broke it with myself." She started to cry again. "I had to tell someone. It had to be you."

Jack's penis went soft. So this wasn't going to be that kind of a call. Marriage to Molly had certainly kept him guessing. "What are you going to do next?"

"What do you mean?"

"You could turn on the ignition and come home. I'll wait up."

"I can't Jack. You know I have to get through this. It's good for both of us, don't you think? I mean, you're surviving, right?"

He didn't know for sure how to answer. If he told her how nervous he felt with her gone, how the ground felt shaky and how he questioned basic decisions, every small action, had allowed a couple of girls to cower him and then consume his days, she'd worry. He and Molly didn't really have the kinds of conversations like the one she was initiating now. She'd think he had some sort of a mini-stroke. And in a way, he was getting by, now that he thought about it. He was doing all right by Mandy May and himself. He didn't want to color her experience with his lame insecurities. She was upset. The program meant a lot to her. She was right. Her journey there had nothing to do with him. But he did want to keep her on the line. He liked hearing her voice as he curled onto his side alone in the dark.

"I'm good, Molly. Mandy May and I are having a blast. I'm reading a great book, a novel, actually. The tomatoes are still going strong in the greenhouse and this afternoon I took some WD-40 to that creaky swing over at the park. I'm keeping busy."

There was silence on the other end of the line. Did he say the wrong thing?

"I miss you, hon."

"I miss you, too, Jack."

"Go ahead and eat my half of the pizza. Then get back in there. You can start fresh tomorrow."

"Yep, that's what I think, too. That's what I'll do."

After, Jack could not go back to sleep. He lay there thinking over his life with Molly, their children, and their grandchildren, this old farmhouse they inherited and lived in, the house they'd probably die in. But they weren't dead, yet, and the world they lived in was the world they lived in. He thought about the tragedies he'd seen and heard about and his friends and the kids of his friends who'd committed tax fraud or died of cancer or divorced or got caught growing pot in the basement. As his thoughts swirled and the sun came up hazy and shining on a skim of snow in the branches outside his bedroom window, he wondered if lying here thinking like this was the same as meditation.

And then there was Molly, dear Molly, who worried that she committed a crime in eating a pizza and that made him love her even more.

The next afternoon, as Jack passed through the park on the way to story hour at the library with Mandy May, he saw a fire truck parked near the swing set and a group clustered around the bench—a jogger talking on her cell phone, two fireman, and a police officer. The bench was a lump of charred wood on an iron frame. Snow dust covered the ground. One of the firemen was holding a can of WD-40. Jack's face flushed and his gut felt thick and cold. The can must have fallen out of his tool belt when he climbed down the ladder. Someone must have used it to ignite the bench.

He gripped Mandy May's hand more tightly. He felt they were being watched. He scanned the rest of the park, the dugout, the line of trees on the edge, looking for any sign of the girls. At the edge of the woods that lined the baseball field, he saw a dark figure, just one of them, Reese, dressed in black.

"What happened, Pop-Pop?"

"Looks like a fire, Mandy May."

"Mary, Mother of Jesus," she gasped, another Molly-ism.

"Let's get going. We'll be late for story hour." He looked back over his shoulder at the barren playing field. Reese was gone.

"It was those girls, Pop-Pop. They were smoking." In her excitement her voice rose, but they were by the slide, still too far away to be heard. "It was like you said. The leaves!"

"Shhh." He pulled her along more quickly. "Maybe, Mandy May, maybe."

Jack was finished with those girls. He was finished with lounging around the park. He was through with his role as morality police. He had been careless. Had forgotten the can and in a way was responsible for the vandalism. He thought about Molly and her detox transgression and how his focus on those girls bordered the threshold of pure unadulterated lust. Everyone was capable of keeping secrets, telling lies, committing misdemeanors. In fact, all of humanity was on the brink of some perfect balance between right and wrong, making tough choices, suffering consequences, living their lives. They walked past the scene of the bench fire and along the sidewalk to the one stoplight in this one stoplight town.

"Let's go and get some books."

But something niggled at Jack as they waited for the WALK signal at the crosswalk. Mandy May was no dummy. There was more he should say about the fire.

"Mandy May, I don't think we should go making judgments and saying things about those girls and that fire unless we know for sure."

Mandy May laughed.

"What's funny?"

"You sound like Mom-Mom."

He arched his eyebrows. "True."

A flock of geese flew overhead. They counted together. Ten of them! The light turned green. They crossed the street and headed to the library. After, he'd take Mandy May up the hill to play at the farm. She could run wild all she wanted to in the apple orchard. He'd fix the swing on the old maple.

From Inside

The girl inside the black bear costume, whose community service job it was to jump out from behind a tree and terrify the night hikers at the Forest of Mystery fundraiser for the nature center, had been stumbling around in the same sweaty suit every night for two weeks. People arrived in carloads and traipsed the woods to get the crap scared out of them by youth masquerading as indigenous species.

Some people came more than once. The stick-thin man with stringy hair the color of corn silk wore camouflage coveralls and orange gym shoes. Claudia studied the man who hiked alone, his head bent to the leafy path. His yellow flashlight illuminated two feet of the ground in front of him, a flashlight identical to the one her father kept in his kitchen drawer for emergencies. And there, the comparison stopped. Her father was buff. He dressed like a catalog model. Her father wouldn't be caught dead alone.

When the man approached her tree, she sprung, snarling. She felt more alive than ever. But the man never flinched. Where was the fun in that?

After the first few nights, Claudia anticipated the man, her goal to catch him off guard. She would pause a little longer or jump a little sooner. She amplified her growl. One night, she crept ahead, stood in the middle of the trail, and refused to budge, which bent the rules. The man stopped just short of bumping into her. Through the suit she sensed the energy of his body.

Claudia flushed, felt foolish, exposed, her arms poised in the air with the potential to grab. The inside of the rubber mask dripped condensation down her cheeks and into her mouth, tasting like hard-boiled eggs. The rasp of her amplified breath spooked her. She stomped to the safety of her tree.

The next day, she signed up for extra black bear shifts, swapped out selling caramel apples for the heavy costume. Her friends cracked up. Who would actually *want* to wear the bear suit?

All of her strategies failed. She needed a better plan, a rule breaker. She'd broken rules before: a lipstick here, a pack of gum there. She loved the high. The bulky Hello Kitty wristwatch had been the risk that led her to community service hours, the scratchy bear suit, and the man.

She considered grabbing the man's arm, but didn't think the awkward plastic pads of the paws would allow it. Instead, she would fling her body into his as if it were a mistake, as if she couldn't have judged the distance properly because of the puckered eye slits. Yes, an excellent excuse.

Halloween night. The parking area in the nearby field seemed dull with sparse traffic. Just before the usual time of the man's arrival, Claudia felt her body tighten. She imagined the way the man might pace himself, waiting until others had gone ahead, wanting to be alone with her in the woods. He would move toward her with purposeful deliberation. Tonight they would speak out of necessity, she thought, apologies and laughter, embarrassment over the run-in.

She strained to hear footsteps shuffle the leaves, her heart a toy drum. She felt the muscles in her legs contract, ready to spring. Was he coming? The man was late. The ache in Claudia's hollow gut spread and rose and lodged, now an apple in her chest.

An afternoon long ago, she was ten, waiting on the porch for her father to pick her up for the weekend visit. She held a Honeycrisp in her hand, all polished up for him. When her father pulled his truck into the driveway, Claudia saw a woman riding shotgun—big teeth, burgundy lipstick, highlighted hair teased in a knot—and leaning into her father's shoulder. She looked nothing like Claudia's mother. She looked the opposite. Claudia heard right away how the car radio blared with country western pop, songs that she and her father hated. The shotgun seat belonged to her.

At her father's house, Claudia practiced how long she could get away with skulking around the living room unnoticed while her father and his new girlfriend danced to Willie Nelson. Claudia felt smaller with each visit. Over time, she found she could disappear right in front of them, a whole afternoon, but soon tired of that. It was a small-change game. So she tested her invisibility on the greater world, haunting the dollar store with her friends on the outskirts of town. Her treasures grew. Whenever she pawed through the cache she hid in her closet—mostly eye liner and lipsticks—the sparkly feeling in her gut spread to her limbs as if the glitter nail polish she liked to swipe ran through her bloodstream.

Tonight, inside her bear costume, her blood felt cold and congealed. Where was the man in his orange shoes? She longed to get the tingle back in her limbs. So she pictured herself the way she wanted the man to see her. Tall, beautiful, hair poised in a knot on her head, deep-red lipstick, a woman. He could see her maturity, her elegance, through everything, and in her mind, the man's hair was clean and trimmed. His clothes were dark and fine, a business suit maybe, his shoes made from Italian leather. Her image of the man's form had shape-shifted into the stature of an athlete, more like her father's, and his gait spread beyond the weak beam of the yellow flashlight.

She felt her arms and legs jittery beneath the rubbery suit. Sweat dribbled the base of her neck. Her thighs ached from squatting. She longed to stand and arch her back.

Gradually, the field emptied of the crowd of parked cars. Night air seeped into the eyeholes of her mask. Her skin turned cold. Tonight, no one she knew had come and the man she hoped for wasn't coming. She wouldn't jump out before him. There would be no flinging.

Claudia crouched down. She remembered the weekend her father failed to appear at all, and the weekend after that, and the next. She rolled to one side and slid deeper in the moon shadow of her tree. She pulled dried leaves around her furry slipper paws, clutched her arms around her middle, and curled. She willed her blood to slow and held her breath. All she wanted now was winter.

Ms. Bellamy

The principal invited Maeve into his slate-gray office. Though he offered her a chair, she remained standing, a soaring five-feet eleven-inches topped with cloud-white hair, her spine as straight as the flagpole in front of the high school. He leaned back in his black leather chair, Tom Bender, a green recruit who should not cost the town much money, and yet a fancy new glass-top desk filled the space between them. Maeve placed her hands flat on the transparent surface and positioned her chin to maintain eye contact. After a few requisite niceties, the principal asked if she would consider taking an early retirement package at the end of the school year.

"It's not that I want to *lose* you, Ms. Bellamy. Everyone *knows* you're the best. We're thinking of your aspirations." He fiddled with the end of his silver tie. "You could finally finish that book you're writing."

Maeve felt disgusted by his forced cheer. She suspected that he, not "we," was thinking of his own aspirations—a man who wore dark Italian suits, a supporter of No Child Left Behind. He had nothing to lose.

She'd heard about his three-year pact with the school board, parents Maeve had taught to write compositions when they were fifteen: carve the high school budget into a sliver, rescue the commodious building from the grip of consolidation, and garner some achievement awards to embellish the front hall.

"The school board would like you to attend the meeting next Thursday night to discuss some options." He leaned forward to polish a smudge on his desk with the cuff of his suit jacket. He would not look Maeve in the eye. She had not said a word.

"You will be treated well, Ms. Bellamy," he said.

Ms. Bellamy. She didn't even make her students call her that. Treated well. Maeve couldn't stomach glossy people. She would get what the state gave anybody else who put money into the pot for decades, maybe a little extra for the buy-out.

"I'll be at the meeting, Tom," she replied, emphasizing the use of his first name; this was a small-town school, after all. "But, I'm not making any promises. I hadn't thought to retire quite yet." She glanced at the looming clock. "Time for senior seminar."

Maeve only smiled at him when she saw that she left behind oily fingerprints on his desk.

Last spring, over at the general store, Wren, sweet Wren, who like Maeve had never married—though at forty-eight, still had time—heard two board members talking at the coffee counter about a possible redundancy, and was surprised, so when Maeve was in for the Sunday paper, Wren warned Maeve of their scheming.

"You were my favorite teacher," Wren said. "I think it's awful, the changes they've made over at the school."

Wren had looked distressed and it reminded Maeve of the time Wren came to Maeve as a young teen, fretting over the SATs. Maeve helped Wren form a study group. Maeve remembered all of her students. She liked no one more than any other, but Wren had lost a sister in the final week of senior year, and Maeve visited Wren from time to time throughout the summer and all of the next year when her family was falling apart.

Maeve cared about all of the kids. Above and beyond, she cared, but that didn't seem to count. Here it was again, a hint of a mandatory retirement. Did the whole town already know about a plan to shove her out, and after all the good years, decades, she had given them? She had only ever briefly considered retirement. She was hardy in health, still generating lively curricula, though since last spring, the seed that had been planted by Wren niggled.

Maeve had heard about these kinds of deals before. Oh, one could fight it, the union backing you, but a teacher she knew who fought long and won spent the next year wondering if everyone wished she were gone. Her teaching went to shit. The next year she retired anyway without the added benefits.

The whole bloody thing felt so Dickensian, as if the specter of an unaccustomed future rose before her. She wondered if perhaps this was how one became a ghost, materializing gradually from the inside out. Maeve had never seen a real ghost, but standing in the flat space of Tom Bender's suggestion, a life outside of these concrete block walls, she felt as if she could become a kind of filamentous wraith, as if the numberless clock on the wall in the principal's office, a steely blank stare, ticked off her recent birthdays . . . sixty-seven, sixty-eight, sixty-nine.

During her final class of the day, Maeve swayed by the window overlooking Town Hill Cemetery as sophomores in Accelerated English II read aloud from *The Awakening*. She had planned on giving students time to read to themselves, but now did not want to sit in a quiet room filled with people, the sounds of pages turning. Instead she allowed the drone of comfortable words to permeate the atmosphere.

Outside, snow dust charged by low sunlight burst across her view as if shattered glass fell from the clouds. She thought that if she did leave teaching for good, she'd free up time to catch more of these tiny miracles of life, perhaps finish the novel she seemed to always postpone.

The bell rang. Bodies scattered. A few students tossed back farewells. Maeve thought it was sweet the way Melissa Wiley always thanked her as she flew out the door. Her older brother had done the same. Now he fought in the war. If she stepped down from her post, here, would she continue to follow the lives of the graduates if she didn't have their younger siblings, and eventually their children to remind her? Would she miss the broadcast of awkward limbs and backpacks in plastic seats, the vibrations of metal chair legs on buffed linoleum?

She draped her black wool coat and red knit scarf over her right arm and cradled a folder of essays against her hip. She clipped the light switch, and fumbled with the key at the door. Locking up was the new rule by the grand new guard. Ridiculous. Who'd want to pilfer a pile of outdated anthologies or multiple copies of *Bleak House*? The principal was an idiot. She shuddered at the tone he cast upon her benevolent old school.

Skip it, she thought. She left the door unlocked. She slipped into her coat and wound the scarf around and around her neck with her free hand, as if securing her head to her body, then laughed at the image. Often, the tenor of her thoughts ran morbid. Often scenes from the macabre infiltrated her private moments where she would write herself into scenes out of Poe or Hawthorne. She sometimes edited her own imaginings. She could lose herself in writing. It was her job that kept her grounded.

On the way out, in the front hall, she waved to Meredith, another former student who grew up and is now the art teacher. Meredith hung self-portraits sketched with India ink by ninth graders. Maeve noticed Meredith's blackened fingers. She paused. Once someone's teacher, always their teacher. "Try white toothpaste and a nail brush."

Meredith stepped back from the wall and glanced up at Maeve. "Excuse me?"

"Your fingers. If you want to get the ink off."

"Oh, right, thanks."

Then Maeve noticed the smudges under Meredith's eyes, the kind caused from sleep issues and grief. She had a strong fondness for Meredith and an urge to take her under her wing ever since Meredith lost her mother. Meredith had always been a person of substance, and now that she was a colleague, was a potential friend. Maeve had few friends. By the time school got out in the afternoon, most women Maeve's age had already been downtown sipping hot drinks and discussing flimsy novels. By four o'clock, they had finished their shopping and banking and were preparing an early supper to eat while the television played on the kitchen counter. They exercised in swimming pools, attended bone strengthening classes, did yoga, had grandchildren, and traveled with their husbands.

"Have a good weekend," Maeve told Meredith. "Get some rest."

"You, too," said Meredith.

Maeve nodded, but she already got plenty of rest, in fact she felt less and less like sleeping. She left the building and crunched across the snowy parking lot to the cemetery.

Maeve knelt in front of her grandmother's gravestone and used her coat sleeve to brush off chunks of dry snow hiding the front surface of the monument.

Marion Birch Bellamy

1900-1973

Maeve always felt close to the spirits of her ancestors. She laughed out loud when she realized that, with the exception of her students, she preferred company with people on pages and in cemeteries. She considered the essence of her grandmother as good a friend as anyone walking the planet.

"Well, Gram. It finally happened. They're telling me it's time to close up shop."

She stood and blew air into her cupped palms, then hugged the folder of papers to her chest. She tucked her bare hands into the sleeves of her coat. She had things to recollect with Gram. The cold could do what it wanted.

Maeve had been called before the school board on odious business three times in her forty-eight-year career. Once was in 1962 to defend *Of Mice and Men*. Some parents wanted it banned from her syllabus for inappropriate language, of all things. No one had said a word about the treatment of women or the word "nigger." Maeve had lost her best friend, Evaline Sullivan, over that one, over Steinbeck for God's sake. People went crazy when they got too wrapped up in their kid's education.

The second time was in 1976. One day, only three out of seventeen tenth graders had turned in their World Lit homework the day after the premiere of *The Bionic Woman*. Television had become a threat to youth and education. At home that night, she dragged her old black-and-white TV into the woods behind her house and shot the thing to pieces with her grandfather's turkey shooter she kept in a closet. News about it spread among students and their parents.

Since she'd done it at home, the board members looked the other way. No one wanted to waste time on hiring committees. Parents liked that their kids read Shakespeare and learned to spell in her classes. Some of them had had Maeve as a teacher themselves. She dressed up as literary characters. She let seniors choose the spring play. That's what got her into trouble in 1989.

The senior class had chosen to perform a series of one-act plays on issues of sexual identity, teenage pregnancy, and addictive substances. A surprising number of community members attended the event. The theatre was so packed, Maeve had to send a couple of fathers for more folding chairs from the church basement and set them up in the aisles of the auditorium. The old principal turned his back on fire codes. He liked controversy. Afterwards, no one left the theatre in hopes that they could find someone else to take issue with the offensive content. The next week: another meeting, another warning.

"Do you remember that night, Gram? I do, like it was yesterday."

To her credit, she had won two State of Vermont Teacher of the Year awards, and was recently honored for her years of dedicated service at a luncheon in Montpelier. She had more than a couple engraved plaques for Excellence in English Teaching on her walls.

Standing in the cemetery, Maeve heard Gram's voice in her head, as crisp as the day's weather. "I think you've still got some of the good fight left in you yet."

Maeve blew a kiss to the headstone. "That's what I think." She trod the snowy sidewalk towards home.

When Maeve entered the front hall of Gram's old house where she now lived with her ninety-two-year-old mother, the entire downstairs was dark. "Mother!" she called up the stairs, flicking the hall lights on.

"I'm up in the attic." Her mother's voice came fluting down the banister like fresh dust. "God, is it five? I'll be along shortly."

"What are you doing up there?"

There was no reply. Maeve headed into the butter-yellow kitchen to warm some leftover soup on the stove and cut brown bread and cheese for their supper. By the time her mother appeared, she had laid out bowls and spoons and poured each of them a glass of the homebrew that her mother still bottled each summer.

"Hello, Maeve." Gwen gave her daughter a light kiss on her hair as if she were still a girl of twelve come home for an after-school snack.

They hadn't always lived there together. Gwen moved in twelve years ago when her husband, Maeve's father, passed away. Maeve couldn't imagine either of them living anywhere else.

"What were you doing up in the attic?" Maeve asked. "You'll fall one of these days."

"You shouldn't worry. I'm up to something, though, something quite wonderful." Gwen smiled and sank into her chair. Her cheeks were pink and her hair moist around her forehead. When she gulped her beer, a froth mustache formed on her upper lip.

"Are you going to tell me what it is?" Maeve pointed to her own lip, mirroring where Gwen needed to wipe. Sometimes, Maeve felt like the mother.

"I'm going through old trunks. I saw in the paper that Evaline and Molly are putting on a vintage fashion show to raise money for the new addition on the fire department. Wren is donating baked goods and coffee from the general store. They put a call out for clothes *and* models. We have some pretty special pieces up there, Maeve. I found two unopened packages of silk stockings. You'll die when you see them. You should help. I always said you'd make a good model with your height."

Maeve pushed back her chair leaving her soup to cool and sipped the warm beer. "Except I'm an old woman, Mother. Who wants to look at scarecrow legs in vintage hosiery?"

Gwen scoffed. "Well I'm not too old. I'm going to see if they'll let me show Aunt Mary's silver fox coat. It's patchy, but no one will see it up on stage. They're using the school auditorium. Having older people model makes it funny."

When they washed the dishes, Gwen asked, "Why won't you help, Maeve? Whatever happened between you and Evaline can certainly be let go by now."

"The First Amendment is what happened between Evaline and me."

"Oh, Maeve." Gwen waved her hand as if she were brushing away flies. "You're always so contrary."

Though Maeve decided it was not a good time to ask Gwen for advice about the question of retirement, she longed for her mother to tell her that, in contrast to her grandmother's advice, it was really okay to give up the fight.

After supper, Maeve climbed the stairs to her office to work on character sketches for her novel based on the townspeople she scrutinized. Sometimes she thought her attempts sounded hollow, feeling that all of the good stories had already been written. If she retired, her writing was all she would have, just a pile of messy pages begging her to give them some semblance of purpose.

On the way, she noticed that her mother had left the light on in the attic. Maeve hated going up there. She had grown up here as a child and the attic stairs still tripped memories that rubbed like scratchy fabric on her skin.

As teenagers, she and her best friend, Evaline, would creep up after everyone was asleep to hunt for ghosts. They clutched each other in their thin flannel pajamas. The beam of the flashlight wavered on an off. They'd wrap their arms around each other's necks, and reach their hands to cover each other's mouths to keep the other one from squealing too loud. Maeve liked the feel of Evaline's cool fingers on her face. Sometimes she'd part her lips and taste soap residue with the tip of her tongue, but not hard enough for Evaline to notice it was on purpose. All

those years later, Maeve still remembered the tang of
Evaline's skin.

Once Maeve had dared Evaline, who was ghastly afraid
of the dark, to stay up there all night on her own, sleep on
one of the summer cots atop the musty goose ticking. She'd
promised to buy her a shiny silver diary with a key if she
could last the night. Maeve told Evaline she'd be in her
own bed, and that she would leave the bedroom door open,
but instead she made a nest on the hard floor of the attic
stairs with pillows and blankets. She knew what Evaline
risked for the diary. Later, she woke up sore in the darkness
to the sound of Evaline sniffling and tossing on creaky
springs. She crept up waving her flashlight to announce
her arrival and slipped in next to Evaline, who had flopped
to one side facing away from her. Maeve set the light on
the floor so it cast an eerie glow on the wall beside Evaline,
but Evaline would not give up her act of irreproachable
bravery. Maeve circled Evaline's waist just below her
budding chest, feeling the presence of the puffed flesh on
the top of her arm. Maeve remembered feeling so much
love for Evaline that night, how all of the skin on her legs
prickled as if she'd walked through nettle by the millpond,
and how her heart muscles pressed on her lungs. She had
thought of how Heathcliff ached with black rage for his
neighbor Catherine in *Wuthering Heights*. She didn't
understand what it meant at the time, how she enjoyed
being cruel and then sliding in to offer closeness in the
dark, how she stayed awake all night listening to Evaline
breathe while she willed herself not to scratch at the itches
caused by the shafts on the goose feathers that jutted
between the weave of the old cot mattress.

Maeve can't imagine what made her think these moldy
thoughts from so many ages ago. After the attic sleepover,
she had thrown herself into reading more, and spent less
time with Evaline. The desire to touch her hair and wrists,

pull her close by her waist and hold on had made both of the girls self-conscious.

Years later, Maeve had had one affair with a woman who wore a man's plaid hat and low-cut shimmering floral dresses. She met her in college while smoking hash from a water pipe at a poetry reading. The woman was an Emily Dickinson scholar and loved sleeping with men, too. After three months, the woman left Maeve to caravan west in a train of Volkswagens. Maeve had called the woman a cliché. She wanted to go home and teach in the same building where she had fallen in love with Austen, Elliot, the Bronte sisters, and Henry James. It was the sixties. The world had become a strange place. The stories were changing, both in fiction and real life, and Maeve loved them all. She lapped them up. But she didn't want to be part of them. She wanted them held safely at a pole's length. Books kept her mind off the things her body had learned from the poet, the slippery feeling of THC in the bloodstream and fingers between legs. She had traded one kind of love for another.

As she reached for the pull chain of the attic light, she thought of the things she had let go—sex, companionship, maybe even marriage and children—and how over the years romance had floated away like an airless raft on the mill pond in the low autumn sun. This was her town, her school. She'd given them her life. No snotty two-faced principal was going to shove her out the door just to turn and wipe his hands with gelled sanitizer from his germ-free wall dispenser.

On Monday morning, Maeve searched her coat pockets for her red gloves before she realized that she must have left them on her desk. She collected the papers she brought home to grade, essays stacked in a pile on the kitchen table from the worst to the best. She never said anything out loud about it, but the students who would get their papers back first knew they'd get a cold stare to go with it. Why even waste my time, her expression asked them? Her job was not to coddle. It was to teach them how to write. Somehow, they still loved her.

When Maeve walked into the front office, she saw her red gloves on the secretary's desk. "How did these get down here? I must have dropped them in the hallway." "Mr. Bender wants to see you, Maeve." The secretary's voice sounded wrinkled.

"Oh, for Pete's sake." Maeve snorted. She felt like a first grader. She slogged to the principal's office.

"Miss Bellamy, I hope you had a good weekend. Did you get some writing done?"

Miss Bellamy was even worse than *Ms.* Bellamy. Maeve was still and silent, like the snowy egret in the brittle rushes she sometimes saw on her river walk to school.

The principal cleared his throat and sat down behind his glass desk. "I wanted to chat with you." He looked at his watch. "On Friday, I checked all of the locks, as usual." He looked at her. "I really need you to cooperate with the new system. We need to cover ourselves in the event of an incident. Do you know what I mean?"

Maeve thought from the look on the man's face that he must be constipated.

"No."

The principal sputtered about break-ins and the cost of new locks.

"What does any of that have to do with my teaching literature, *Tom*?" Maeve imagined her neck looked as pink as a plucked chicken's, a flush that always gave her rage away. She turned, stormed out of his office, and retrieved her red gloves.

On her rush up the staircase to her classroom, she met Meredith, all swallowed up in her down jacket. She clutched a box lid filled with small clay pots. They stopped in the middle of the stairs. Maeve saw that Meredith's fingers were clean.

"It worked," Maeve said, pointing. "The toothpaste worked."

"Yes, thank you." Meredith's face was bright, like pink tulips.

Maeve leaned back on the stair railing to even up their height and said, "May I ask you a question?"

"Sure."

"You've known me a long time. Do you think I seem like one of those teachers who stays on past her time, you know, starts to lose it on kids, or forgets people's names and who wrote *Macbeth*?"

"I don't think so. I mean, you've always been everyone's favorite as far as I know. I think you seem quite with it or something."

Maeve bent her head back. She stretched her neck from right to left. "Yeah, I have to work on keeping my cool with that new guy, Mr. Slick."

Meredith's eyebrows flew up. "Not so sure about him, are you?

"Not sure at all. Do you want to get coffee after school some time? I've been wanting to catch up ever since you came back to town."

Meredith relaxed her brow and licked her upper lip. She scratched the back of her calf with the toe of her boot. "Sure."

"Good." Maeve nodded. She took the rest of the stairs two at a time. "That's very well and good," she called to Meredith from the top of the stairs.

The afternoon before the school board meeting, Maeve and Meredith met for coffee at The Little Red Hen. They talked about the things they held in common. They both graduated from Amherst College—Maeve's advice for seventeen-year-old Meredith to attend—although when Maeve graduated it was still just for women; they both liked to read ghost stories, old ones and new ones, loved Shirley Jackson—Maeve had introduced Meredith to *The Haunting of Hill House*; they both enjoyed theatre and small concerts in pubs. Maeve asked Meredith if she wanted to ride down to Amherst together for a play one weekend.

"That sounds nice." Meredith wiggled her nose. "Let's see." Then she looked at her watch and said she had to run.

After Meredith rushed off, Maeve sat alone for a half an hour or more feeling the warmth of a rekindled connection linger across the table. She imagined the shape it would become if it could become flesh, a fruit, pear-like and smooth, something that when seen in light would create shadows and depth. Maeve liked to think in metaphors and felt satisfied that the pear image rang true of art, Meredith's specialty. Maeve wondered if she and Meredith would talk about more important things the next time they met.

At the meeting in the school library, Maeve sat at the end of a long table showing Meredith and Wren a book of portrait photographs by Walker Evans, their heads pressed together like schoolgirls. Temperatures outside had slumped below zero and the heater was humming. Maeve still wore her black coat. She had planned to hear the school board's offer and scurry home to join Gwen for a frosty beer in front of the woodstove, discuss her options with her mother, and retire early with a new novel. Now she felt she could stay out all night. She felt proud and alive. Not fresh, the way she felt that night in the attic with Evaline, or victorious, the feeling she had around the sex-drenched poet, but more like a student feels on the first day of a new school year, with a matching outfit, a well-stocked pencil case, and a couple of new friends.

She was so intent on the camaraderie she felt alongside of Meredith and Wren, she didn't realize how the room had filled up. When she looked around, the library was packed. People stood at the edges of the room; some were sitting on low shelves, their dangling wet boots clunking the books. Thick jackets were piled everywhere.

So much for executive session status for discussing personnel matters. Word must have gotten around town. Maeve imagined the town had come out to support her contract for another year. At least she thought that was why Evaline had come. Earlier, Maeve had run into her in the front hall and Evaline invited her to participate in the fashion show. Her grandson was with her. Sky was one of Maeve's graduates from the past spring. She had asked Sky if he was looking forward to seeing his old teacher waltz down a runway dressed liked Daisy Buchanan. His presence diffused the tension. They'd all laughed as if there had never been a riff. A silk scarf the color of spruce set off Evaline's long, creamy throat, her skin like a girl's. Maeve leaned and pressed her cheek against Evaline's in a self-conscious hug.

"It means a lot to me, Evaline, that you came out tonight," she said.

"You've been one of our best teachers, Maeve. Of course, I'd come."

"Still am one of the best, I certainly hope."

"Still are," said Sky.

When Sky touched her arm, it had taken the sting out of Maeve's displeasure of being referred to in the past tense, but now Maeve wondered what Evaline meant by her comment. "We'd better go find good seats," Evaline had said and pulled Sky along.

Maeve looked at the clock—a normal clock, white face, black rim—on the wall above the librarian's desk. The meeting was supposed to start at seven and it was quarter past. People were talking louder and louder, about anything and everything as far as Maeve could tell.

Tom Bender walked in wearing a gray tweed overcoat and a slick haircut. He draped his coat across the back of the chair at the head of the room, but remained standing. He kept pulling at the knot of his tie. Maeve watched him glance around as if he were looking for someone. She watched him find Meredith. She turned and saw Meredith meet his smile. Meredith flushed coral pink. Were the two of them a thing? Maeve felt her limbs fill with a thudding weight. The purpose of the meeting, Tom had told her, was to discuss options. Now it seemed odd to Maeve that all of these people would be here to hear about Tom Bender's decision. She realized that man was up to something underhanded, the likes of which this innocent town may not have seen coming.

Tom flashed an open-mouthed grin and clapped his hands together with authority. "Okay, everybody. Let's go ahead and get started."

Maeve watched Tom make grand sweeping gestures, heard the strum of his speech—the river of time, the importance of story, the collective history gathered here—but at some point she stopped listening to his words, so clouded were her thoughts about their purpose. People of all ages stood and shared memories of Maeve, how she could recite the majority of Whitman off-book, how she made the freshman class wash their hands with soap, and then sniff-tested them, before she passed around her first edition copies of Salinger and Fitzgerald on the opening day of high school. Yet between each and every speaker, Tom inserted his own comments about the need to keep the school strong by building new rooms and shoring the foundation, keeping the school moving forward. So when there was laughter over the blown-out TV incident, in Maeve's head it sounded canned, like someone was making jokes on a sit-com. Was she the only person in the room to discern the subtext? He somehow made it seem like he and she were on the same team.

She perspired beneath her coat, felt drips fall between her shriveled breasts. She felt the way she did as a little girl when her mother threw her a surprise birthday celebration and invited people she didn't like. They played parlor games that she hated. She'd only ever wanted Evaline and a trip to the shore. Tonight, even though she knew she didn't want whatever this was, she wasn't exactly sure what she could do about it, but she was certainly grateful she had not brought her father's turkey gun along. On bitter nights like this, she could still feel the ghost of the recoil pain in her shoulder from the day she shot out the TV.

When they finally called her name, Maeve placed a hand on Wren's shoulder before she rose out of her chair. She watched the Ryans—Sky, Molly, and Jack—stand as a group, clapping, an ovation. They still wore their coats, too, and it dawned on Maeve that all of the people wearing their coats could have been as easily standing by her grave as in this library.

She wound her way through the throng. Applause wrapped around her, pulling and pushing. Tom Bender was a snake. He'd set her up so she had no choice but to accept such a great honor to allow forward movement with dignity. She felt herself become thinner and thinner. People patted her back. Their touch pummeled her through her coat, her skin, her flesh, until reaching her bones.

When she arrived at the front of the room, expected to make her remarks, she turned and looked out at the crowd. Faces looked mute, like the India ink sketches on Vellum in the front hall. She reached into her coat and felt her gloves, one in each pocket. She remembered. She had refused to lock her classroom door. She could refuse this path as well. Though the library was silent except for the hiss of the heater, Maeve's head pounded.

"Thank you for your kind words and for coming out tonight in this ghastly cold, though I am not certain what we've accomplished by doing so except to have warmed this hallowed place with the heart of community." Maeve heard phrases come out of her mouth in the bass tones of her dead grandmother. It was Gram who said things like *hallowed place* and *the heart of community*. Maeve could not see Gram's ghost, but she was sure of her presence in the room, pressing her to take a stand, one way or the other, for her rights, or for her freedom.

"Your support is noted and appreciated, as is the trust you have placed in me with your children and grand-children." She glanced to where Evaline sat with her family.

"I've watched many of you grow older and move on and come home." She smiled at Meredith and Meredith smiled back.

"And I've seen your children grow." She looked at Molly, who blew her a kiss, giving Maeve a girlish feeling. "I've treated them with the same care and respect as I would have treated my own children, had I had them."

Meave pulled her gloves from her coat pocket. She held them before her, lined them together, and grasped the pair in her left fist, all the while casting a glare at Tom Bender who looked down at his polished shoes, then out at the community, and then to the floor. She placed her right palm against her chest and could feel her heart beat even through the thick wool of her coat.

She turned her attention back to the crowd and smiled. "It's because of your enduring faith in me and my concern for the students, the one and only reason I've kept at it all of these years, that I'm not certain we, as a town, are quite ready to clean out the old guard entirely, not just yet."

Here, she looked out at Wren to see her clasp together her hands and shake them above her head in a symbol of victory, a gesture Maeve associated with her Gram.

"I hope for your continued support in whatever path I decide to take for next year." She faced Tom Bender, who was loosening his tie. She willed a steely expression.

"I will let my decision be known to you, Tom, in the morning."

Maeve expected the thunder of more applause, though none came. She felt flush with heat in the silent room, more than a hundred eyes on her next move. Class was not yet dismissed. She took her time, pulling on one crimson glove, then the other. She glided out of the library into the dimly lit hall. Wrapping her scarf around her neck and covering her pillowy hair, she narrated herself walking away, as if she were writing a story. Tomorrow she would announce her final decision, Friday, her favorite day, after Accelerated English II class and *The Awakening* read out loud.

Accommodations

Wren mopped the scuffed up floors of the old general store to the beat of Bob Marley and the Wailers. As she sloshed gritty bucket water on the linoleum in the end aisle, she peered through the glass storefront. January snow had turned to sleet. A Chevy Silverado pulled in and stretched long and black like a hearse aside the lone fuel pump in the lot. Its driver, a rusty-bearded man, about her age, she guessed, fiftyish, got out and tugged on the nozzle. He wore no hat or coat. He looked towards the entrance. He reminded Wren of a Van Gogh self-portrait, scowling and grainy through the spattered glass. A floodlight shone on the fuel pump island framing the scene like one in a snow globe, but the fixtures were odd—pump, truck, man— in place of little cheery cottages with shrubs.

The man walked towards the store pointing at the truck and shrugging his shoulders. Wren had already shut down and locked up the store for the night. She had been looking forward to a good storm, getting home to a glass of Scotch and some time off her feet, and though she shook her head and mouthed *we're closed,* the guy wasn't getting back in his pick-up. She gripped her mop as the man walked to the doors and rattled the double handles. He'd left the truck running. His headlights tunneled an opaque glow down the main road towards the busy section of town. Skidder rose from the rug near the bakery table and stretched his decrepit mutt legs and Wren felt comforted by his presence. He limped to join her as she walked slowly towards the door. She saw now that it wasn't a bad temper shaping the features of the man's face, but sorrow, an ashen pallor she'd seen on other faces, dozens of faces amidst the hundreds who'd passed through these doors, an expression she had seen in her own mirror. Still, a small smile from the guy would have eased her concern.

"We're closed." This time she hollered through the glass over the rhythms of the reggae. Skidder wagged his tail. "Some watch dog you are," Wren muttered, placing a hand on her dog's head to settle her heebie-jeebies.

"Do you know where the nearest gas station is?" he shouted. "I'm running on fumes and a prayer out here." He flipped his collar to shield his bare neck. He cupped his hands and blew into them.

Stark Run was small enough that the station on the other end of town would be closed on a Sunday night as well. The man seemed harmless. His clothes resembled what her father used to wear to his law office, a creamy broadcloth shirt, neat jeans, and brown Oxford's entirely unsuited for the weather. But she was anxious to get home. If she let him in, she'd have to turn everything on, see to the man, then turn everything back off, and mop over his tracks when he left.

Recently the therapist who Wren worked with around her anxiety issues looked at her over the rim of his thick black glasses when he told her that, without question, she was an accommodator. He said it as if she had a potentially terminal disease and needed to understand its severity. He went on to tell her that she needed to examine why it was difficult for her to say "no" to most people and "yes" to herself. She needed to figure out why she sabotaged her ability to go out there and try life by exhausting herself in always giving to others. For starters, she had to practice putting her own needs first.

During her last appointment, Dr. Stewart assigned her to think about the present from the vantage point of an envisioned future. *What do you want people to say about you when they look back over your life? Try and zero in.* She'd been giving it some thought. She couldn't seem to nail it, but she took what he told her to heart: if she kept on giving to this town, she'd still be mopping floors at eighty.

The man at the door moved his hands from the handles to his pockets. "Won't you help me out?" he pleaded. Shoulders hunched, a skim of ice topped his cinnamon hair. He seemed tired and cold.

She let him in. She knew the multiple risks she took by doing it, and she still let him in. She imagined Dr. Stewart shaking his head and pushing his glasses up the bridge of his nose as he sat back in his red leather chair.

The stranger craned his neck to scope the aisles as if he were looking for someone. She scooted behind the counter to re-activate the pump and cash register and felt safer with the barrier between them. Skidder nose-nudged the man's thigh.

"So, just the gas," she said. "Go lie down, Skidder." She jerked her chin towards the rug near the bakery table, but Skidder only wagged.

"Do you have any coffee going?" the man asked rubbing his hands. "I've been driving since just lunchtime without a break. And could I use the restroom?" He bent to stroke the dog behind the ear. Skidder leaned his head into the man's hand and groaned.

"I'm sorry. There's no coffee. In theory, we're closed." Wren felt more secure speaking in the plural, as if there could be a burly husband in the backroom. "We just cleaned up. You can grab a drink from the cooler. The restroom is back behind the DVDs."

The man disappeared into the bathroom. She wanted to finish mopping the last aisle, but remained at her post behind the counter near the telephone. She had left the mop and bucket by the door. She could wipe up the man's footprints after he was gone. Something about the Jamaican beat pulsing the air seemed off. She flipped through CD cases to keep busy, glancing at the aisle that led to the back.

Before she could choose a new CD the man returned to the counter, pink-skinned and combed, as if he had given himself a paper towel bath. He pawed through a pile of wrapped baked goods. He picked up a scone and smelled through the plastic. "You wouldn't happen to have a microwave, would you? This looks like it would be just the thing if it were a little warmed up. I'll just go grab some OJ," he added. He glanced out the window at his truck.

"Sir, the store is closed. I'm anxious to get home safely. Why don't you go pump the gas while I heat this and then we both need to hit the road?" She talked fast. Wren was surprised that she automatically kicked into using Dr. Stewart's Three Steps to Making Respectful Requests: state the situation, attribute a feeling, form the *need* question. She used a firm, clear voice, maybe a bit too firm. That tip she picked up from dog training.

He backed away from the counter pressing his hands down as if attempting to soothe her. "Okay, I get it. I'm moving."

At the toaster oven, through the glass of the deli case, she scoped his movement. He prowled the back of the store, then stood staring into the cooler. She thought of TV shows that ended with the mild-looking well-dressed guy turning out to be psychotic. If he was low on fuel why did he leave his truck running?

The Bob Marley CD ended. The sudden silence pulled his presence nearer than his actual location in the store. She felt relief when the microwave bell rang.

"You're scone's hot," she called out. "The fuel pump's on. Could we speed this up?"

When he set a half-gallon carton of orange juice on the counter, she noticed his hands were shaking. "Is this your store?" he asked.

The inkling of danger, now palatable, twisted inside her stomach. The tightness in her gut rose to her chest. Dr. Stewart had taught her to manage these first signs of a panic attack—breathe in, one, two, three, and release. Why was he asking her this question? Why didn't he get on with filling his tank?

"It belongs to my family," she answered. "My husband should be here any minute to pick me up." She'd used a made-up husband in the past. "How much gas do you want?"

"I'll fill it. Can I leave a credit card?" He pulled out his wallet, opened it and stared at a wad of cash, but didn't remove any of it. "I need help."

Confused, Wren waited. He seemed to have plenty of money and several credit cards. Did he need help counting the money? She glanced at the portable phone safe in its dock.

"There's a story to all this." He handed Wren a credit card, eyes still looking into the wallet. "You must think I'm insane. I'll try and keep it simple." He ran a hand through his wet hair and finally made eye contact. "My wife's in the truck. She's sick. Pretty sick. Dying actually. She's asleep now, but I'd like to wake her and bring her in. Maybe see if she needs to use the bathroom. We've got a ways to go tonight. We're heading to Maine."

"Wow." Wren glanced outside, running the plastic card against the edge of the counter. The border of Maine was a solid two-hour drive and the truck was now frosted in a capsule of sleet. "Look, I really am sorry, but this is getting a little weird, and the roads are turning to crap. I'd really like to get home."

She circled the heel of her left hand against her third eye as instructed by Dr. Stewart to help stimulate clear thinking. "But I'd like to see you settled for the night. How about you go pump gas, and I'll make a phone call." She swiped the card through the machine and set it on top of his wallet. She took a twisted comfort in the fact that if her body were discovered later, mutilated in the backroom, at least the cops would have a tangible record of the killer. What was she thinking? He said he had a sick wife. She massaged her temples with her forefingers.

"We have a nice innkeeper nearby who makes a wonderful breakfast. She always has an available room and a pot of hot soup and bread in the kitchen. The place is spotless. How does that sound?" Wren reached for the phone.

The man lunged across the counter and grabbed her arm. "Please! No." He looked as terrified as she felt. He released her shirtsleeve and backed away. "Just wait a sec." He turned to face the window. "We're not going to make it to Maine. I don't know what to do." He looked back at Wren. He walked to the door and leaned his forehead against the frosted glass. His hands formed into fists at his sides.

"We should call an ambulance," she said, her throat thick, her mind trying to discern the truth of the man's story. The situation went well beyond the extent of any advice from Dr. Stewart.

"No." He spoke into the glass. "No ambulance. No hospital. No supports. She made me promise." He turned to face Wren, leaving a clear oval on the clouded window. A thin drip of condensation slid down the glass. "She's a nurse. She's seen too much *sterile suffering*, as she calls it. I promised. It's the only thing she wants. That and the

Atlantic Ocean." He smiled and Wren witnessed spousal love in his soft expression, the kind her parents had shared when she was young, before her sister's accident, before all of their lives took a tragic turn. She looked away so not to intrude on the man's privacy or perhaps she looked away to protect her own heart. So deft she had become at shutting off the valve of her own pain.

She could only guess what the travelers had in mind. Was he to place her into the sea and let the waves sweep her into the icy night forever? Did he have a brown vial of a lethal substance in the glove box of the truck? Was he going to hold her as she fell unconscious with pain? Wren didn't even know the woman's name or illness. The story might not be true. It was as though she were in a stage play among actors without a script.

Skidder stumbled over and put his head beneath the man's hand. Wren sighed. Dogs knew how to act in times of trouble. The man squatted and rubbed the dog's neck, jingling the tags on the collar. He buried his face in Skidder's silky fur. She knew the comfort a person could find there. Sleet blew and shattered against the window near the cash register.

Wren's sister, Anne, had attended NYU. On her way home for Wren's high school graduation, she was killed in a traffic pile up on I-91 outside of Hartford. At the end of the funeral and the gathering for refreshments, when all of the well-wishers left the house and her mother went up to lie down in Anne's bed, Wren sought her father and found him standing on the porch with their chocolate lab. It was as if her father and the dog were anticipating Anne's return, her car pulling into the driveway, and an explanation as to why she was getting home so late. Wren eased herself through the screen door and approached her father. She put her hand on the back of his shirt, clammy with perspiration. He turned to her and said, "Oh, hey, kiddo. How are *you* doing?"

"I'm all right," she answered and maneuvered his arm around her shoulder. She felt him study the top of her head.

"You didn't get to graduate, Girlie," he said, squeezing her shoulder and leaning to smell her hair.

She warmed whenever he used her kindergarten nickname. She liked to hear it the way she liked his homemade strawberry pie on her birthday and him reading Dickens aloud at Christmas. "It's fine, Daddy, really."

She gazed at the empty field up the hill past the yard. "But I have decided something. I'm not going to go to school in Oregon. I'm going to stay home for a year or two with Mom. I'll take classes at community college and help out."

She looked up at him. He seemed to scan the horizon for ghosts. He answered, "I think that's probably a good thing. Give yourself some time." Though Wren didn't *want* to give up college before she even got there, he was saying that he needed her too.

The following spring, her father quit his law practice and moved to Honduras to install safe water systems. Wren understood. Life flew out the windows of the house when Anne died. Her mother lay on the couch most of the days, getting up to shower, sip wine, and look out the living room window most of the nights. Wren convinced her to sell their place and buy the store when it came on the market. Running a store was something she knew that they could manage together. Five years later, her mother moved to Albany to help an aunt after a stroke. Wren moved into her grandmother's place, a small house that stood empty about a mile out of town abutting the cemetery. From there, she could walk to Anne's grave whenever she wanted. Wren didn't see her parents much. It was as if coming together would bring them too close to the grief they'd hoped to forget.

◆   ◆   ◆

Skidder scratched his underbelly with a back paw. The man stretched up from his crouch. He looked out into the night. "I know it's a ton to ask, but I could use a friend and it looks like you're it," he said. He opened the door. Frozen air shuffled the weekly flyers in the newspaper stand. He glanced over his shoulder. "I'm going to bring her in."

From behind the counter, Wren felt the tears pool in her eyes, as she squinted at the man shuffling across the parking lot. He carried a tiny woman in his arms; she could have been a child. She was wrapped in a white and blue-striped blanket. The night, dark and bitter with sleet, seemed to be ushering them towards the building. Wren rushed to open the door.

The woman was cocooned except for her face. She appeared somewhat younger than her husband, beautiful, with pale skin, bright lips, and course black bangs that framed gray eyes. Wren recognized the visage of death in the wife's expression, as if a part of the woman had already crossed over. They exchanged a smile. Wren felt shy. "Hello. Come in," she said. The woman's eyelids closed.

Skidder lifted his head and thumped his tail on the floor, but did not get up.

"She hasn't talked much lately. I'd like to take her into the bathroom," the man said.

"Of course." Wren looked around for a place where he could set her down. "Follow me." In the café corner, near the back of the store, Wren shoved two square tables together to form a rectangle long enough to make do. "After, you could bring her here to rest." They both spoke as if the wife weren't in the room.

"I'm Wren," she said.

"Wren. Thank you. My name is Forrest," he said. "And, this is my wife, Anna."

◆　　◆　　◆

Anna. Not Anne. Still, it was close enough, the difference of one letter, one sound. A chill ran through her. Wren realized she was involved in the kind of bizarre story that she heard people discussing over coffee and muffins most mornings at the store, often surprised at how much drama played out in their quiet town. Only this time, she was the main character, not merely providing the set. What she would say and do would affect the outcome of the lives of the other players.

She searched the back room and found a wool blanket, and a couple of five-pound bags of rice. She crafted a makeshift bed, thinking that the woman might want to stretch out after being cooped up in a truck. She wished she could provide more comfort than this, but then again, she thought, she ran a store, not a hotel.

Murmurs hummed through the bathroom door. She could not make out words. She walked to the front of the store and looked out. Forrest had turned off the truck. He still had not pumped the fuel. While she waited, she did her breath exercises. She couldn't shake the nerves, or rid the dull feeling in her chest, though the feeling was not the same as fear. She made coffee and warmed up two more scones. When in doubt, fix food. She warmed a can of soup from the shelf and made sandwiches. She bustled about as if there were a line of people waiting on lunch.

Forrest and Anna were taking forever in the bathroom. In the café area, Wren set a smaller table next to the longer table for their feast. It occurred to her that Anna was probably not eating much, but she didn't want to act as if the dying woman wasn't to be considered.

When Forrest brought Anna out, he still carried her; apparently she was past walking. Wren watched his eyes rove around the spread of food. He shook his head. He positioned his wife onto her side on the long table and curled her in a spoon position. When Forrest propped the bag of rice under her head, the blanket slipped off of her shoulder. Wren saw only bones and yellowish flaking skin where Anna was not covered by a hospital gown. The woman's pink knuckles protruded like swollen boils. Anna looked just like the hospital patients interviewed on a documentary Wren had seen a couple of years ago on television, middle-aged women who struggled with anorexia, a little-known phenomenon.

Wren shoved the food to one corner and covered it with the edge of the tablecloth. She watched Forrest. He pulled a chair up as close to his wife as he could, sat down. He perched his elbows on his knees and dipped his head into his hands.

Wren didn't know if she should speak. What was the extent of the man's torment? Was he praying? Her sister Anne had not asked her family to enable her death. She lost it to fate, leaving her family with questions. Wren never got to say good-bye. How could Anna have asked her husband to help her do such a thing? Yet, here he was, and willing to assist. Was this one of those deep and powerful loves that went beyond the boundaries of death? Wren had foregone love like this for the most part. When her young heart had been smashed early by grief, her life closed up tight, like the insides of this store in winter, but seeing the tender look on this man's face, the way he ached for her, made her want to do whatever it took to get the hell out of her rut and see if there wasn't something else out there for her. She'd have to think about that later.

"Forrest," she said. "I don't think it's too late. She could get help. We should help her. The hospital is only twenty minutes away."

Forrest shook his head. Anna seemed asleep. The corner of her swaddle, the blanket, had the words *Property of Green Hills for Women* stitched with red thread into the soft wool.

"She's come from a facility, hasn't she?"

"It was a residential program, a whole setup for women in varying stages of the disease. It's rare in women Anna's age, but I'll be the very first one to tell you, it exists."

He spoke as if they had already named the disorder out loud and Wren couldn't figure out if they were making separate yet similar assumptions about what was happening in the store, or just sailing together without a compass into some psychological underworld.

She knew she should question her own limitations, let him know how far she would go to help them before she felt compelled to act out of urgency. At the same time, she wanted to leave space in the conversation for the other to come forward and act, another skill she was practicing in therapy. She didn't always need to provide solutions, or fix things, or say something to ease all hurts, her therapist had told her. Dr. Stewart called this behavior a distraction tactic that Wren used to keep from dealing with her own issues. He asked her to afford room for others to come around to their own answers and that they might come up with a resolution that wouldn't involve her giving away her time so easily. If she could allow that to happen, she'd have more time to figure out what she wanted for her own life.

"Anna's been in and out of the place for years," Forrest said. "When she lost her nursing license last year, it was pretty much over in terms of a will to get better. She'd been at Green Hills full-time for six months when she took off. We couldn't find her for three weeks. She was brought back in an ambulance. She'd been camping in Utah and was discovered by hikers. She said she wasn't planning on dragging me in to it. She wasn't even going to say good-bye."

A sand truck rumbled through the stillness of the parking lot. Her neighbor from across the mountain often scraped a swath through the parking lot with the town rig to save Wren some money on private plowing. Wren fantasized racing out the door with Skidder and catching a lift home from Addison, leaving the strangers to find their own way, but she thought of her sister Anne, who died on a highway, hours from home and family. No one had any way of knowing Anne's final thoughts and wishes, or the extent of her pain. She stood and waved through the window to thank Addison. Addison honked twice.

Forrest scooted his chair back, turned, and pulled back the tablecloth from the food. He picked up a sandwich. "Hell, I don't have any trouble eating."

"No, of course. Please eat."

Wren sat down with Forrest while he ate two sandwiches and sipped a cup of warm soup. Skidder stared at him with round polite eyes that said, I love you and I love your sandwich. Forrest gave him the last crust.

"How old is he?" Forrest asked as he rubbed Skidder's chest.

"He's thirteen. Getting up there."

"He seems like he's in pretty good shape."

"He's got lymphoma. I'm managing his pain. I need to make a decision pretty soon about how far to go with that." She cringed when she realized she'd just compared a dog to a wife.

"Well, we've got something in common," he quipped as if reading her mind.

She felt no judgment in the awkward joke. Who was she to tell someone how to deal with death? "It sounds like it's been a long haul."

He nodded and leaned back in his chair. "In my imagination, I've been through as many possible deaths, or worse, as she could have had during those weeks that she was missing." He wiped his eyes with the back of his quivering hand. "I can't even cry anymore."

Wren scraped crumbs from the tablecloth into her hand and dumped them on a plate. "Are you sure it's too late, and you're positive that this is what she wants?"

"I'm afraid so."

"And, she wants to get to the beach?"

"To her grandmother's house on the coast."

"Is her grandmother there?"

"Yes."

"And, her grandmother knows."

"She knows. Anna grew up out there."

Wren understood how important it was to be able to say good-bye. No matter how suddenly a person died, or how long they were dead, having a chance to see the body, touch the hair and skin, get over the shock and numb of coldness like no other, a person remembers that forever.

"I think you need to keep driving. Try to get her there. Stay here a minute. I'll bring you some more coffee." Wren stood, cleared the table, and dumped all of the dishes in the kitchen sink behind the deli case. She checked her computer for the weather and road reports for New Hampshire, the stretch of highway between here and the coast. The sleet had tapered to a light snow and the main routes were sanded. The skies were to clear by midnight.

When Wren returned to give Forrest the road report, he had scooted his chair around to seat himself next to his wife on the table. He leaned over her, his face close to hers, his back hunched. He was murmuring in her ear. As she drew closer, Wren could see the shape of his back and shoulder muscles through the stretched weave of his shirt, how his body seemed ready to spring with activity and it occurred to her how he was far too young to be losing a beloved wife. What a tragedy, it seemed, how a person's body could be taut with vitality, yet his spirit so weakened with loss, and how the spirit trumped when showing wear on a body's mortality.

"Don't worry, sweetie." He spoke softly. Wren took a few steps closer. "We'll figure something out. I'll keep my promise. I'll get you there."

His shoulders began to shake. Wren stood holding a fresh cup of coffee, but could not bring herself to interrupt. He needed her, but what should she do? She pictured herself helping him get Anna settled into the truck, supplying drinks and snacks, words of encouragement, but could not envision how Forrest would be able to tend to Anna while driving. Wouldn't he want to hold onto his wife during her final hours? And if Anna were to die along the way, he would need a great deal more support than a brown paper bag filled with sandwiches.

Forrest and Anna's predicament was not unlike other problems that came through the store: a berry farmer forced to bludgeon a deer tangled in netting while her toddler watched; a family made homeless after an electrical fire from an old air-conditioner reached the propane tank which exploded and took half of their trailer with it; a single father left alone to witness his son, home from the Middle East, spiral into an opiate addiction. Over the years, she'd served up hot coffee and listened to a host of woes. She'd opened early, stayed late. So, yes, she was accommodating; what was so bad about that?

If she sent the couple on their way, she'd stare out the window wondering how they fared. If she let them stay, she'd worry about the grandmother in Maine, Anna and the grandmother both bereft of that final good-bye.

Forrest seemed too overwhelmed to choose a path. Wren suspected that when he had walked into the store carrying his wife like a child, he crossed a threshold he believed would offer some relief like the others who crossed the threshold of the store before him and had been doing so for more than the hundred years that this store stood.

She retreated back to the counter. She pulled a thermos from the lost and found bin, washed it with soap and warm water, and filled it with fresh hot coffee. She provisioned a brown paper bag with more sandwiches and chips and candy bars and gum. She wrapped herself in her coat and scarf, pulled her hat over her ears. Outside, the Silverado was crusted with precipitation. She set the picnic sack and thermos on the driver's seat and found a scraper in the back. She chipped the crust of ice from the windshield and calculated that a full tank would get them to the coast.

When she finished, she felt heated and flushed with a rare vibrancy achieved only from night air following an ice storm when a person stood outside and imagined the rest of the town tucked in, cozy in their beds. She looked through the window into the store. She saw what Forrest would have seen, the overhead lights doming the aisles of food and supplies, the basic staples she stocked, the promise of warmth and sustenance an oasis.

Inside, she turned off the pumps. She left a note on the counter for Molly who opened up on Monday mornings. She grabbed Skidder's leash. As she approached the table in the back she saw that Forrest held Anna's leaf-thin wrist in one hand and rubbed the old dog's ear with the other.

She whistled. "Come on, pup." Skidder wagged. She clipped the dog's collar to the leash. Wren leaned and squeezed Forrest's shoulder as if he'd been a customer for years. He turned from his wife to meet Wren's eyes. He smiled. "Thanks for all of your help. You've been great."

"Tell Anna . . . call her grandma. She'll be there in two and half hours, tops. I'll drive."

Mabel, Mabel

Saturdays at our house can be sad and mean, although no one does anything on purpose. My older sister, Emily, and her boyfriend, Sky, sleep and sleep until the silence in the house wraps around my neck. When they finally get up, they feel too sick from Friday night beer games to write papers for community college. They lounge and talk about what they should be doing instead of doing it.

It made my mom crazy when people wasted the day. Our brother, Cooper, was an early riser. Now he volunteers in Liberia. On Saturdays, my mom and Cooper used to bring Emily and me chocolate chip pancakes in bed at dawn, then dragged us out to places they'd read about in the paper-—a recycled art festival or a book swap, things that were cheap or free and usually more fun for my mom than us. I had a hankering to go to Ice Cream Castle, just once, and sit on the red velvet chairs you can see from the street and eat the breakfast sundae named "Fit for a Queen" from a fancy glass dish with scalloped edges. I'd seen the ad for it in the paper. My mom said it was too rich for our blood, and then she laughed, but her eyes didn't.

Now it's Emily who takes care of me while my mother tries to get better at a retreat for people getting off pills.

Our father lives in Boston. He can't even pick up the telephone. Emily and I visit our mother every Saturday afternoon. I read teen vampire books to her. When it's time to go, she puts her hands on either side of my face and tells me that she'll be home in no time. I feel something like a small mouse in my throat and focus on swallowing, so I won't cry.

It's thirteen days until my twelfth birthday. I keep track on the Three Stooges calendar by the telephone in the kitchen. The counters are a mess from last night: beer bottles, open bags of chips. I grab the fat black marker from a drawer to cross off the day before it actually starts. It makes the time go faster. One squeaky thick X over Saturday.

Today, when I visit my mother, I'll find out if she'll be let out in time for my party. She's never missed my birthday. Emily has told me not to count on it and not to worry, that she'll plan something fun. But I don't want a pizza party and virgin Jell-O shooters. I want little carrots sticks and red grapes and homemade cheese puffs and all the stuff Mom knew how to make in the kitchen that she kept clean and shiny. I know Cooper would come if he could.

My best birthday was when I turned five and Mom redecorated her office into a room of my own. Purple wall paint and white trim. A gauzy canopy above my bed. She stood back when she was finished and smiled in a way that she sometimes smiled, like it came up from the inside. Cooper gave me a scrawny gray kitten that cracked us up, how she kicked her legs in the air. I named her Goat. My own room and a fuzzy kitten. The best birthday ever.

Last month, I got a job at The Little Red Hen to escape the Saturday morning house. In the laundry closet in the kitchen I pull a rumpled skirt and a damp sweatshirt from the dryer. I dress in front of the washing machine, throwing my nightgown on the dirty pile on the floor and grab an open bag of corn chips from the counter. I go out the back door. Grainy snow, slush really, lines our driveway and turns the brown grass into icy mush. The chips are stale, so I sprinkle them on the lawn and wonder what to do with the bag. I avoid the trashcan against the fence because of the crows all lined up on top, their mean black eyes, and their scaly legs. Pesky beasts, my mother used to say, but gave them our stale bread. They're here even though she's not. I hate them. They want and they want. They flutter down to poke at the chips and I drop the empty bag to pick up later. I jump the four concrete steps to the sidewalk to get that tingling feeling in my feet and legs and run down the street and away from the house.

At the bakery, Mr. Bartlett is setting up sticky buns in perfect rows on a shelf inside the glass case. Looking out, he makes a fish-face like he's in an aquarium tank, which would have been hilarious if I was six, but I smile back so I don't hurt his feelings. I tie the strings of an apron around my neck. It falls below my knees. I fill an old plastic lard container with hot water and lemony soap in the sink out back. Then I scrub the wooden tables and benches by the picture window in the café area. When I was little, I sat there with my mother and traced the tip of my pointer finger along the curled shapes of letters and words carved into the varnished wood. Now I feel them through the thin wet cloth made from a flour sack.

"Good morning, Miss Mabel," says Mr. Bartlett as he pops his head out from inside the case.

My name isn't Mabel; it's Charlotte, which is just as bad. I don't remember why he calls me Mabel—some silly childhood thing—and I've never straightened him out, so I smile and wave my dripping cloth towards him, feeling the tickle of water on my wrist.

"I've saved the biggest bun for you and you know where to find it."

I set the bucket down on the counter. My gigantic cinnamon bun sits in the back room, warm and steamy. I eat it faster than my stomach can handle and for the rest of the morning, while I fill up the napkin holders and sugar jars, I walk around with my stomach puffed out past my chin.

A few hours later, when a customer orders soup, I know that at home it's time for lunch, time for my sister to wake up and stand under the shower so she can drive me across town to the retreat. I could walk, but Mom made my sister promise she'd drive me there and home again until my twelfth birthday. Twelve is the age you can visit your mother without a grown-up.

I say good-bye to Mr. Bartlett's pregnant wife, who has been working in the backroom, and now leans against the cash machine, her bare arm propped up on the gray metal looking like gobs of dough in the mixer. Through the opening in her sleeveless dress, I can see the saggy skin and white shiny streaks that fold into wrinkles on the side of her hanging boob. My mother wears a tidy white bra. My sister's bras are the color of candy wrappers. I have nothing there yet, but one night a few weeks ago, my sister looked me up and down when I was drying off from my bath and she needed the good mirror to put on her mascara. She told me she could tell my boobs were coming. Any day, she said, as if they would pop out all at once. She bought me a sports bra at a yard sale, but who wants to wear someone else's underwear?

Mr. Bartlett asks, "Are you going to see your mother today?"

I nod and he hands me a warm hard-boiled egg already peeled. "Tell her we say hello." He gives me a greasy white paper bag that I know holds two fat slices of pepperoni pizza, one for me and one for my mom. She loves to eat it cold in her room at the retreat.

"Thanks." I stuff the whole egg into my mouth and roll my tongue across its slippery surface. I grin at both of them with the egg pushed into one cheek, and then switch it over to the other and they laugh. It's the same every Saturday. They seem to enjoy how they can count on me for the small things I do and for making them laugh. For a whole morning, it's like I have parents.

Outside it's warm, like spring instead of February. Customers call the quirky weather *global warming*. I feel free not wearing a coat. Other kids ride bikes in the high school parking lot, or weave around cones on skateboards, but I stopped hanging out with other kids when my mother stopped sleeping nights and left marks on her arms with her fingernails. When she picked all the hairs out of her eyebrows, I freaked out and called my sister, who lived with Dad and went to college in Boston. She came home and took care of everything. That was last fall.

Emily says that one reason our mother is so anxious is because Cooper lives in a place full of poverty and sickness, a place where the Internet is always down. Sometimes I study the atlas at school, the page on Africa. It helps me feel closer to him.

A couple of the kids riding their bikes wave me over. My arm twitches, but I pretend I'm watching a crow perched on the bench who eyes my bag of pizza.

When I get to the house, it's quiet. I get a doughy feeling in my gut because I know we're going to be late. I set the bag with the pizza slices on the kitchen counter and climb the stairs thumping extra loud on the creaky boards. I hate when I have to wake her up. The bedroom door, where Emily sleeps in my mother's bed, is ajar. Inside, it's dark and smells like the yeast Mrs. Bartlett puts in the mixer. Emily is sitting up, facing the wall. Her long brown hair streams down her naked back and disappears into the quilt around her hips. She begins rocking up and down. She turns slightly and I see that her eyes are closed and that a large hand is clutching the white skin of her back. The hand belongs to Sky, the boyfriend. I understand what I am seeing and turn and slam the door shut.

I hurry to my room and lie on my bed with my legs running up the side of the wall. I lift my shirt and place my fingers above my ribs to massage my dull heart. I begin to thump the wall with my sneakers, leaving angry gray tracks. My cat flies out from under the bed and into the open closet. Now my heart pounds and I feel like I exist. I run my hands down to my full, heaving stomach. I don't like the thought of the bakery as much as I do when I first start out hungry in the morning. I listen to the shower running in the bathroom on the other side of my wall. My head feels sleepy thick. I doze off and on.

Emily strolls into my room. She's wearing a tan summer dress and I can see her black bra and red thong underneath. She uses a Chinese chopstick from an old take-out carton on my dresser, dried rice and all, to wrap her wet hair in a knot above her neck. Her armpits have black hair stubble caked with gross white powder. My mother would have never flashed her armpits.

"I'm ready to take you now, Charlie."

No apologies. I follow her downstairs and search under the couch in the living room for my good shoes. She goes into the bathroom.

"Whatcha' looking for, Charlie?"

It's Sky. I turn to look up and hit the top of my ear on the sharp edge of the couch where the upholstery tacks are coming undone. It burns and I feel blood trickle into the little cave in my ear. Sky chomps the crust of a slice of my mom's pepperoni pizza from the bakery. Goat has peed in my shoe. Emily waltzes in, a baggy sweater over her dress. She's wearing leggings and muck boots. She smiles as she brushes her teeth, foamy mouth and all, as if nothing bad is happening.

We arrive on my mother's floor fifteen minutes before the end of visiting hours and are told that she is not up to seeing anyone today. I imagine all my bones crumbling to mush inside me like crackers in soup. Emily hands me six quarters. "Go get a snack from the machine in the lobby. I'll see what I can do. Meet me back here in five minutes." She kisses my forehead. I smear it off.

I ride the elevator down with a man about the same age as my brother Cooper, but this guy's as thick as a refrigerator. He scowls at the closed doors in front of us. I lean against a wall to one side. He is wearing a blue-gray short-sleeved uniform shirt that says, *Maintenance.* I come up to his elbow. He has a snake tattoo that must end on his shoulder because the part I can see is tailless, slithering down the side of his arm. The head wraps around his wrist like a real snake would. It's drawn in 3D, and extra creepy. The snake man smells like Sky's shaving cream. I step back to the corner of the elevator. He crosses his giant arms, and I see more tattoos, red and blue angels, but then I hear a bell and the door slides open. He leaves in front of me and the door almost closes before I remember to jump out.

I've missed the lobby and find myself in the basement. The elevator door closes behind me. When I try to get back on, I can't find a button. The bun and egg I ate earlier have worn off and I need to pee. I look up and down the hall, but I am afraid to move away from the elevator in case I get lost or miss a chance at the door opening. My mother is in her room somewhere above me wondering why I'm late bringing her pepperoni slice that Sky has already eaten. I hear footsteps coming from around the corner and the snake man is back. He clumps towards me like a big black bear. He would make a good security guard. Thinking this helps keep my mind off the fact that I peed a little in my underwear.

"Want a lift?" he asks and swipes his card in the barcode reader. His voice is like Tom Waits, the singer that Sky plays off his computer. Tom Waits sings about bars and trains, and Sky tries to imitate him while he swirls and dips Emily, who smiles and goes along with it, the grimy dish towel hanging from her hand. When they do this, I feel like I should be somewhere else, but I don't know where, like I'm trying a locked door.

The snake man and I stand next to each other in the elevator like before. "Are you lost?" he asks. He reaches out and pushes L for Lobby.

My mother always told us to be wary of strangers as our town was changing. But what am I going to do, just stand there like I can't hear? "I forgot to push the floor I wanted." The quarters are sweaty in my hand. I still need food and I'm moving from foot to foot to stop the pee.

"What floor do you want?"

"I'm getting off in the lobby." I get an idea. "You work here, right? Would you happen to know my mother?" He shrugs. "Who is she?"

"Moira Cook. Fourth Floor. Room 407." I use a tall stately voice like a lady in a book. If I respect him, he will respect me.

"Nope."

"They won't let me in to see her today."

He nods his head to the beat in the iPod buds stuck in his ears. I'm not even sure if he hears me. I tug on his snake arm.

"Yo," he says.

"Do you work here a lot?"

"Too much. What do you want from me, little sister?"

Little sister. That's what Cooper always called me because he knew I didn't like my name. The night after my first day of kindergarten, Cooper found me in my secret place in the closet where I used to hide with Goat and a flashlight. I'd sit in there with my legs stretched up along the wall and look at all of the Sunday comics I had saved in a folder. I remembered what my mother read and then told myself the stories over and over. That way, alone, I could look at the pictures and know what the people were saying. Cooper crawled in next to me because I was late to the dinner table.

He asked, "What's all the fuss, Gus?"

"I hate school."

"Who doesn't? But, kindergarten's got to be the best part about it." He danced his fingers in front of my flashlight making shadows on the wall. Bunny ears stretched out long and creepy. He was using up all of my oxygen. I kicked the closet door open wider. I didn't feel like getting out. Cooper didn't usually pay me this much attention. "I have to write my name. I hate my name. There are too many dumb letters."

"What do you wish your name was?"

"I dunno. Zoe has a z and that's a cool letter. She can already write her name."

"I get that." He handed me the flashlight and started to back out. "I'm afraid you're stuck with your name, Little Sister." He said the word little and the word sister as if they began with upper case letters. He said it like a title. From then on he never used my name, Charlotte, or my nickname, Charlie. I wonder where Cooper is right now? In the elevator, the snake man called me little sister, but without the upper case letters.

"I need someone to get a message to my mom," I say.

"Do you now?"

The elevator stops and we get off at the lobby. The doors slide shut behind us. "Tell her that I came today and it wasn't my fault that I was late. Tell her I got her pepperoni pizza from the bakery, but that Emily's boyfriend ate it. Tell her that the Bartletts said hello and their baby is coming any day." I grab his arm and he stares at my hand until I let go. "Tell her that it is only thirteen days to my birthday and I want her to throw the party."

"Whoa, slow it down, little sister."

I put my fingers on my temples and press, the way I've seen my mother do when she's had a bad day, just before she started picking out her hair. I think he'll lumber away before I can make him understand, but I can still see his giant black shoes. My head feels thick, my mouth pasty. My stomach spins like I'm rolling down a hill. I look up. The snake man turns into all eyes, small and black like crows, twenty or thirty eyes. I start to wobble. "What if I wrote it down for you?" I whisper.

He grabs my elbow to hold me up and the snake seems to wiggle off his arm onto mine and wrap its way around my skin. Something is wrong. I hear a bell. The elevator. My sister appears and slaps at the snake, screeching, "Get the hell away from my sister."

But the snake-man does not let go. Emily's hair is wild and flying out of the chopstick. Her mouth is spitting.

On the carpet in the lobby, I fall to my knees and clutch at my stomach. I curl over on to one side and see my sister pushing the snake man, who stoops to support me until I am all the way down. Then he lets go and stands. His legs are like two towers above me. I feel like they are both trying to take care of me, but the room is foggy, then black, and I can't tell them about each other.

I wake up in the emergency room. Emily and Sky are there and Mr. Bartlett, but not my mother or Cooper. My sister looks sad, her hair is in tangles and her face is streaked with mascara. She needs the good mirror.

"Hey, Charlie." She strokes my hair like I'm the

neighbor's dog. "You fainted. We called for help and they brought you here, but you're fine."

Sky stands behind her, smiling at me, eyes sparkly, and I forgive him for eating Mom's pizza. He rubs Emily's shoulders and she beams up at him. She is lucky to have someone to love her like this. Cooper is lucky in Africa, not knowing that anything bad is happening. Mr. Bartlett is lucky because he has a wife and a bakery. He can eat whenever he wants. The snake man is gone. I wonder if he went looking for my mother for me. I want him to walk in the room and say something in his Tom Waits voice.

Mr. Bartlett walks over to the edge of my bed. He hands me a balloon from the hospital gift shop. Silver and pink. A ballerina mouse printed on the front. "Hello there, Miss Mabel."

"Who's at the bakery?" I ask and let go of the balloon, which bounces on the ceiling. I'm too old for balloons.

"It's closed. It's nighttime. You already did all my prep work for tomorrow, so I have nothing left to do." He shrugs. He's just being nice.

"Where's Ms. B.?" I ask.

"She's home. She's asleep."

Then Mr. Bartlett does something he's never done before. He leans over and plants a kiss on my cheek scraping me with the whiskers on his chin. "You get some rest, Miss Mabel."

My eyes start to water. I feel stupid, crying. Then, I remember. Mr. Bartlett has rubbed his cheek against me once before. My mother used to take me to the bakery for a muffin when I went to the kindergarten across the street. He would join us at the table in the picture window. My mother drank tea, while I picked the sugar crumble off the top before eating the gooey center.

One day, I was sitting with my arms propping up my chin, slurping milk from a straw. Mr. Bartlett leaned over, pressed his stubbly cheek to my ear like he was going to tell me a secret and chanted, "Mabel, Mabel, strong and able, get your elbows off the table." That's why he calls me Miss Mabel.

In the hallway of the hospital, Emily talks to a doctor and comes back to tell me that we can go home. In the car, I stick my head out the window to feel the strong wall of air slap my cheek against my teeth. I think about my mother. I want to try and figure out what went wrong. I want and I want. I feel my eyes all gritty and dull and the next thing I know Sky is carrying me to my bed where Goat has left hairs all over my pillow.

It's been a week since the Saturday I fainted. Six more days until my birthday, until my mother gets better in time to get things ready for my party. I dress quickly by the kitchen sink for my job at the bakery. Emily has bleached my sneakers to get out the smell of cat piss and I find them stacked on top of my clean clothes on the dryer.

We did not have a beer game party last night. Instead, we cleaned the house from top to bottom. Sky came over with Chinese food and offered to scrub both of the bathrooms, which he did. He left at eleven, kissing Emily at the door like it was a first date. He hasn't slept over with my sister in my mother's bed, but I'll bet he'll be back and I don't mind so much. I sense there's a big surprise afoot. Emily has washed the sheets, but she still sleeps there, probably to throw me off about Mom coming home.

At the Little Red Hen, Mr. Bartlett is behind the counter, fiddling with the coffee machine. He calls over his shoulder, "Morning, Miss Mabel. How are you?"

"Mr. Bartlett, I remember."

He turns to face me, yawning and sniffling. "What's that?" The room fills with the burnt nut morning smell of coffee.

"Fix me a cup of coffee. We need to talk." I plan to tell him I am beyond the Miss Mabel game.

His eyebrows fly up.

"Please," I add.

I get my bucket ready and scrub the table although it is already spotless. Mr. Bartlett comes over and sets a mug down in front of me. "Thank you," I say.

The coffee is the color of the map of Africa on the atlas in the library, lighter than what Emily drinks. I take a sip. It's milky sweet, like ice cream I ate last summer with Cooper. I sip again and out of nowhere come the tears, and I can't make them stop.

"What is it, Mabel?" Mr. Bartlett asks as he climbs over the bench and wraps a heavy arm around me. He smells of flour and maple syrup.

"I don't know," I choke out.

The buzzer on the big oven rings.

"Take your time, Charlie." He ruffles my hair and heads to the back room.

Charlie. He called me, Charlie. To him, I'm just like everyone else with a real name. I thought it was what I wanted, to be treated like the rest, and he is still kind in his tone, but the rock in my chest just got bigger; it's more than I can take. I leave the shop without saying good-bye.

When I get home there is a note from Emily. *I'm at school to work on a paper. The nurse called and said not to come in today. Mom isn't up for visitors. I'll be home soon.* I climb upstairs and head straight for Mom's room. I crawl under the covers on the bed. It smells like Emily, not yeasty anymore, but like her shampoo and a dryer sheet. I close my eyes, and in my head I beg my mother to come home in time for my party.

I think about the snake man. I get up and go to my own room where I write a note to my mother. I walk all the way to the retreat. I know they won't let me in to see her, and if they see me there alone, they'll tell Emily. She doesn't need more worries, so I wait outside in the parking lot. I kick at the grit from the town sand truck. If I can convince the snake man to get the note I wrote to my mother, she'll read it. I know her. If I remind her she'll be there. I start to get hungry. It's been over an hour. Emily will be home and worried. The snake man doesn't appear.

Today is my birthday. The temperature is back to normal, cold, and it's supposed to snow. Goat sits on my dresser near the window flicking her tail at the crows outside. Emily has said nothing to me about a party. It's probably a surprise. My mother will be here when I get home from school and there will be carrots and red grapes and those little cheese puffs that Mom always makes. Cooper will find a way to Skype in.

When I jump the stairs, three at a time and run into the kitchen, I find Emily at a clean kitchen counter making breakfast. Singing, she hands me a teetering stack of twelve chocolate-chip pancakes, with a blue candle from the dining room candlestick in the center. The whole pile teeters and drips with syrup. We laugh and eat from the same plate until my stomach could burst and the school bus driver honks the horn outside. Emily grabs my coat before I run out the door and pulls me into a scrunched-up hug. "Bundle up." It's what Mom would have said. "Happy Birthday, Charlie."

When I get home after school, there is a note on the kitchen table. *Mr. Bartlett called. He wants you to stop by to talk about your job. Pizza with Sky later? Maybe a movie?*

Sure. The party is at the bakery and the Bartletts are in on the whole thing.

I change into my good dress and notice that it is tight across the chest and shorter than last winter when I wore it to a Christmas party. Maybe my boobs are about to pop out. I run all the way to the store and amble in with a big grin. But Mr. Bartlett is alone, tapping numbers into his calculator.

"Charlie! Good to see you. Long time no see." He gets up and gives me a bear hug, my second awkward hug of the day.

"You wanted me to stop by." The guests are probably all hiding out back.

"Yes, Charlie. Trudy and I have been talking. We want you to come to work behind the counter for a few hours on Sunday mornings. With Trudy pregnant, I need some help and you're the best one we know for the job. You're already trained."

I can't believe he's carrying on the plan to trick me. His face is super serious.

"Sure, that'd be good. I have to ask my mom when I see her."

"Oh, it's okay. We already talked to Emily and she said it would be fine."

The inside of my stomach feels like a lump of dough that slowly creeps up to the bottom of my throat. I understand that my mother is not coming and that the people I love are not hiding in the back room. Mr. Bartlett walks around the counter and brings out a white box tied up with string. "This is for you," he says. "Happy Birthday!"

I try to smile.

He says, "Open it."

I set it on the table by the window and he cuts the string with the knife he keeps on his belt. Inside the box are a dozen cheese puffs, like the ones Mom always makes. The smell reminds me of her and I ache to see her holding out the blue plate she has served them on since I was three. The cheesy smell is thick inside my nose. My head starts to hurt and I need to get out of here.

"Thank you for the cheese puffs, Mr. Bartlett," I manage to say though my throat is low and gravely. "I will see you tomorrow."

I don't wait for Mr. Bartlett to answer, but can feel his eyes on the back of my shirt. Plodding along the sidewalk towards home, the bakery box becomes heavy, the lid flapping without the string. When I see my house up ahead, less than a block from where I stop, I feel too tired to carry it the rest of the way. I walk to the bench at the corner. I set down the box and press back the lid. They look just like my mother's. Emily must have given him the recipe.

Mr. Bartlett is a nicer person than I am, but twelve is too old for cheese puffs.

I have money of my own in my pocket. I'm taking myself out for an Ice Cream Castle birthday sundae.

A crow lands on the bench, first one, then another, and another. I back away and watch one of them jump down next to the box. He pecks at the string, and then sticks his beak straight into the box, stabbing at the puffs. The others join in. They want and they want.

The Air of Joy

Ruby left him two days after the winter solstice dance at Town Hall, where a man on a motorcycle, Carl, from up in Bellows Fall, asked Ruby to dance and in turn she asked Addison if it would bother him if Carl drove her home. It was past midnight and the world did not end as the Mayans had predicted. She told Addison that she wanted to feel the air of joy on her face.

That's what she had said, verbatim, *the air of joy*. Huh. See, he might think something like that, *the air of joy*, but he would have never uttered it. Ruby said it like it was perfectly normal. She stood there with the pink sheen of the exercise on her skin and that smile—perfect teeth, and the plump lips he loved to kiss, lips like he couldn't find on any other woman. He wanted her to be happy. She knew Carl from work. What was the danger? Sure. Take a ride on that bike. Wear a helmet.

Later, at home, he brushed his teeth at the sink while she soaked in the tub. He asked her if she had had a good time on her ride. She hummed and closed her eyes. He waited for her in bed, tried to stay awake, but now he couldn't tell you for sure if she had come to bed or if she slept in the guest room down the hall like she had done a lot back then.

The next morning, she brushed his arm with her arm as they passed in the kitchen, not in a gentle way, though, or as if it were an accident. It was more like she wanted to start something.

She yawned. "I think I will just watch movies today," she said. "All day." She arched her brow.

"That sounds nice," he said.

"Or, maybe I'll read a book."

"Even better."

"Why? Why is reading a book better? Are you judging me?" she asked. "You're always judging me. You're so strange."

Addison knew he was a little tough on women because the two girlfriends before he married Ruby had mentioned it at one time or another, that he was unfeeling, that his thinking was strange, yet on the inside, he felt all kinds of feelings; on the inside he felt perfectly normal.

The times when he felt strange were times when his wife Ruby placed his strangeness under microscopic scrutiny and tweezed him with her critique. Save your nitpicking for the bovine parasites at the lab, he thought as she ranted, but he couldn't muster the words aloud. It upset him. Wouldn't he have liked to tell her off, just once? Call her a bitch, a fucking bitch, or rat her out for wearing those drooping shirts and low-slung jeans at forty-nine with her pasty flesh. His mind would allow it, but he couldn't say something so nasty, or see the good it would do either of them.

"Talk to me, Addison." She stamped her foot. "Are you judging me?"

"I'm not. I guess I thought you were saying something else."

"What did you think I said?"

"I can't remember what I thought you said."

"You can't remember. But you just thought it. Like, five seconds ago."

"Right. And now I can't remember."

Why would he care less if Ruby read books or watched TV? He already felt the closing in his throat as if he were a boy heading out to play in the snow and his older sister had tied his scarf too tightly. Once, a kid, at the old public swimming pool, he had nearly choked to death on a peppermint. He remained calm like he had been taught in school. He pointed to his throat. His friends got help and the lifeguard saved him.

That day, standing there in the kitchen with Ruby going at him, he remembered thinking that if he could just point to his throat, she would rush over and give him the Heimlich maneuver and his truth would eject out onto the table. *Fucking bitch, leave me the hell alone*, and the like, his true feelings for them to look at together.

From past experiences, he knew the best thing to do was to leave when Ruby started her wind up. They had agreed in a counseling session, the whole team—Addison, Ruby, and Dr. Stewart. It was best for him to just walk away. It was his signal to her that he could not bear any more of her tirade. Her job was to take the cue and find her quiet place. Dr. Stewart had said that the group decisions made outside of the drama held water inside the drama. But Ruby did not stand there and fuel the argument. Instead, Ruby walked away.

That afternoon, the phone rang. Addison thought it odd that Ruby took the call out in the woodshed without wearing a coat. Then he got busy fiddling with the Havahart trap at the kitchen table and forgot all about it. She came back in with an armload of wood and left the portable phone out there.

The next morning she was gone. Addison couldn't find the phone for days. He didn't miss the phone. He rarely used it. In the same way, he didn't miss the sound of his voice attempting to transform his thoughts into the proper words outside of his head. Weeks later he discovered that he didn't miss Ruby that much, either. Perhaps he was unfeeling and unusual. Shouldn't a man miss his beautiful wife? By the time March rolled around, the divorce was final. Without kids, it had only cost the price of filing papers at the county courthouse.

All of that seemed like a long time ago. Ruby eventually married Carl. Addison had gone on some dates, had a few one-nighters, but mostly, he liked the quiet up on the hill. And he just started something up with an old high school pal, Wren, who used to be sad all of the time, but now seemed brighter and brighter every day.

So what the hell did Ruby want? She had called him up. Addison got a message on his answering machine that she wanted to come back to the house and talk. She wanted to show him her new Harley. Huh.

Addison felt the spaciousness of his current life reduced at the thought of Ruby's visit. He'd made his peace. He'd found his stride. He liked sipping lattes from the new espresso machine over at the general store, or staying for supper at Wren's house after he delivered her firewood or dropped off her syrup. Wren, with her llama and a blue-eyed cream-colored cat, never indicated that she thought there was anything wrong with Addison. Not even once. She liked to talk about the butterscotch flavor of soft maple syrup. They could sit and talk or they could listen to the sound of wood burning in her kitchen stove. How he loved her stove, a Waterford Stanley she had had shipped all the way from Ireland. That was a thing he could understand.

Wren still repaired her own socks when the heels blew out. She wore clothes that met in the middle leaving a man something to wonder about as he drove home. He liked Wren. He was quite certain he would never want to call her a bitch. And now, Ruby, after all of this time, wanted to come for a visit.

There was a word for that. When you picked up your pieces and pulled together your loose ends, ready to fall into a different woman's smile, and then the unexpected something came crashing in, like when you were sipping your coffee at dawn, staring out the window at the last of the snow on the hay field, and a junco collided into the glass of the window. You splashed coffee on your lap. The bird broke its neck, just like that. What was the word he was looking for?

Addison heard Ruby revving her bike in the valley before she rattled the bridge at the brook and rounded the bend in a huff of dust by the sugarhouse, so much dust, that at first, he thought he had misunderstood and that Ruby had brought Carl along. But she was alone. The Harley was spanking new and Ruby on her bike—her silver helmet and her black leather jacket—shone in the sun against the brown hills patched with stubborn snow. Ruby jumped off and lifted her helmet. She waved her hair free, like a scene from a commercial for shampoo only her hair was cut short and the color of blackbirds.

"Hey, Addison."

"Ruby, welcome home."

Now what made him say that? Sure, her smile had lifted him. Then she bent to fiddle with a strap and he noticed her black leather pants and Harley rider boots, orange embroidered flames flaring from the lacing grommets. This was not the Ruby he had met and married down at Town Hall in her Laura Ashley gown made from something she simply had to have, dotted Swiss, nor was she the same Ruby in the honeymoon hay wagon, her hair spilling down her back like the bouquet of daffodils in their wedding photos.

But, okay, people are allowed to experiment. Addison himself sometimes felt the urge to spend a year living in the city attending plays in small theatres and shopping for a day's worth of food at a time or just riding the subway to the end of the line and back. He knew there were things he could fly off to see in the world. He had learned to like Wren's lattes, for example. They were similar to coffee milkshakes, though he didn't understand why a person would drink one every day.

While Ruby fiddled, Addison allowed Wren to slip into his musings. He realized that Wren gave him a lift that didn't sink shortly after; his chin physically lifted. She was steady. He felt fresh when he thought of Wren and that feeling was what he imagined Ruby would call *the air of joy* on his face, so how about that?

Ruby approached the house where Addison stood in his stocking feet on the granite stoop. She pushed up on her toes and kissed him on the mouth and walked in as if she'd just gotten home from any normal day working at the clinic.

The kiss didn't do anything for Addison either way. Huh. He rubbed his lips. He followed her. She threw her leather bag and leather jacket on the cherry dining table. He could hear the studded buckles scratch the new finish he'd applied and buffed to perfection just last week.

"Oops, sorry," she said.

He moved her bag onto a chair and picked up the jacket. "I'll just hang this up for you in the mudroom."

"Okay, I'm going to make a quick phone call."

In the mudroom, as he lifted the jacket to a hook, he smelled marijuana. Not the stale oily lingering scent left after smoking it, but fresh herb, similar to catnip growing wild on the edge of the field in summer, but earthier. He squeezed the pocket of Ruby's jacket and felt a lump. He reached in and pulled out a felt cloth that unfolded to reveal a sandwich baggie stuffed with small buds, reefer, and a pipe made from blue and green whorled glass. He held it up to the light from the window and admired the handwork in the sun. He'd smoked pot quite a bit in college, but never from a pipe like this. He wondered how it worked. Ruby and he had never smoked pot together.

He brought the pipe to his nose. He liked the way it smelled, and how it made him feel, as if he could try something new and different, too. Marijuana was practically legal now. Maybe he would ask Ruby for some of the seeds for his garden.

"What are you doing in my pockets?" Ruby said. She leaned against the doorjamb. "Oh, whatever. Bring it in, Addi-o. It'd be a blast to smoke you up."

Addi-o? She talked like a teenager. He wrapped the felt kit back together and tied the satin string. He was about to put it back when Ruby huffed and strode towards him, her boots clunking across the tile floor.

"Give it," she said and grabbed the pouch from him. "I'm lighting up and you can take it or leave it." She smiled and walked away from him into the kitchen.

Addison sensed the room around him shrinking by the minute. Since she'd been away, the space she previously allowed him had expanded, gradually over time, and because of that, with her here, it now seemed like the ceilings of the house had been lowered. He wanted to feel comfortable again, to fit, but fit into what? He never actually felt like himself around Ruby. He'd figured that out after she left.

He wasn't at all sure why she was here now, but since she was, he wanted to find out what she wanted. She'd been his wife for nearly two decades. Neither was faultless. It took two to do the cha-cha, his father had always said to his mother, and he agreed.

He followed her into the kitchen where she sat on a stool at the island, tamping weed into the pipe with her pinky. She looked up. Her smiling eyes looked like the old

Ruby but that was it—Ruby's eyes in the face of a stranger. She lit the pipe and drew in the smoke. She offered the pipe to him.

He took it and sucked in as if it were the inhaler he sometimes used for seasonal allergies. His lungs opened to the harshness of the smoke, different than the chalky backdraft from the woodstove or the sweet steam from the syrup pans. He coughed twice. Ruby laughed. He took another hit, held it in, and closed his eyes. It all came back to him, how he'd loved smoking dope with his college friends at the waterfalls. He exhaled.

When he opened his eyes, there stood Wren, outside, peering in at them through the kitchen window. At first, he thought she was a mirage. But, no, she stood there wearing her wool barn jacket instead of her parka, a sign of the warming days. She actually waved to them holding up the hoof pick she had borrowed from Addison last week. He panicked and stuffed the pipe into the pocket of his jeans.

"It's Wren!" Ruby waved back. "Come on in, Wren. Come in."

Addison remembered that Ruby and Wren had been in the same book group and would sometimes walk together on the road with Wren's llama. Addison and Wren hadn't talked much about the split up. Stark Run was a small town and Wren would have gotten all the news down at the store. That's what he liked about Wren; she didn't pick at him. She didn't prod and persuade. She let him be.

At the window, Wren smiled and waved and shook her head. She blew them both a kiss and set the pick on the windowsill. Addison watched her walk away, past the bird feeders, and it occurred to him that he had forgotten to fill them with seed that morning. He felt a flutter of emptiness in his gut when she was gone. He felt his fingers on the glass in his pocket sting from the heat and cupped the pipe harder. The THC had begun to take effect. He'd often heard that pot now was different. His socks felt loose on his feet. The crown of his head floated as if it were separate from his brain. He imagined that the words that had been trapped in there started to arrange themselves into messages he wanted to spew out to hurt Ruby. *Fucking bitch, fucking whore, leave me the hell alone.* But the words felt disassociated from the anger. They fell flat, useless.

Ruby got up from her stool and opened the refrigerator door. She stood staring inside the refrigerator like she used to do at night before bed when she was restless but not really hungry.

"What do you want, Ruby?"

"I don't know. What do you have?"

He pulled the pipe from his pocket. It had extinguished itself. Addison set in on the counter.

"I mean, why did you come back?" He washed his hands at the sink and told himself that later he needed to put the hoof pick back in the barn or he would forget all about it and have to tear the tack shed apart looking for it later. He wondered how much Wren had seen and what she thought.

Ruby shut the refrigerator door and walked over to him. Her boots made her taller than she used to be and Addison felt that his linty wool socks made him appear old and vulnerable. She wrapped her arms around his waist and pulled him close. He felt the pressure of her head on his shoulder. She sniffed against his neck. Is this what she did to draw Carl in back in the day? Is this what she did?

"I need to say something to you, Addison. I could never find the right words when I was here. I want to explain."

Ruby couldn't find words. Huh. The notion seemed impossible to Addison. In Ruby's embrace, he let his arms hang by his side. He opened and closed his hands into fists.

"Hold me," she whimpered.

No, he thought. No, no, and no. Addison took Ruby by

the shoulders. He stepped back. A low afternoon sun flashed through opening clouds and glinted through the kitchen window. Light struck the copper bottom pot upturned in the dish drain, catching Addison's eye, and he thought of the word he had tried to remember earlier. Blind-sided. And he thought it funny, the strangeness of this moment, every thought, every observation, heightened. He chalked the whole thing up to dope.

When a cloud scooted by and masked the intensity of the sun, cool air followed and flowed in through the cracked window. Addison felt awake and aware and alive. He raised his free hand to massage his neck out of habit, but his throat felt perfectly open. He still held onto Ruby's left shoulder.

"Just tell me, Ruby. What did you come here to say to me?"

"See, Addison, this is exactly what I'm talking about. I'm trying to stay calm, to be nice, but you're like a slab of granite, or a machine." Spittle flew from her lips. "You're cold. I was freezing to death in this relationship." Her voice raised and he recognized his former wife by the height of her eyebrows and the flailing of her hands as the motion served to fuel her rage. Then she collapsed to the kitchen floor and began to sob into the wooden planks.

This behavior was new to both of them. It was unlike the Ruby he knew who had displayed anger, yes, and disgust, yes, and impatience, yes, but never this kind of gut-twisting grief. He knew he should have felt something, too, but, strangely, he didn't.

Her leather clad legs and feet sprawled, helter-skelter. Her black t-shirt rose above her waistline. Addison observed all of this as if he were watching a woman in an art film. He saw the tattoo of a blue polka-dotted white butterfly on the upper curve of her hip. Something about the butterfly caused him to bend and place a hand on her back. Otherwise, he felt little at all for Ruby. Too much time had passed with too many unspoken feelings from his side. What was the point of airing them now? The small amount of marijuana he inhaled was wearing off, but the lingering scent in the kitchen gave him courage. He felt the boldness he had felt in his youth.

"Ruby, sit up," he said. He stretched to grab the yellow chicken tea towel from the counter, a thing that she had once loved, and handed it to her. He knelt beside her as she dabbed her face. "What's this all about?"

"Why did you say I could go?" she asked.

Addison's thoughts clouded. "Go?"

"At the dance." She kicked the heel of her boot on the floor for emphasis. "You said I could go with Carl." Three more kicks.

Addison rubbed her back and took a deep breath. He had never considered why. He was surprised that she was asking. Hadn't she wanted to go? It wasn't like her to say she wanted something if she didn't.

"You looked happy, I guess. I don't remember."

She nodded. She draped the towel across his thigh. He smoothed it with his free hand feeling the dampness, her tears.

"We made choices, Ruby," he said, his thoughts still muddled. "We both made them. You took action. You were the brave one. You were always the brave one. You tried and you tried. I didn't know how to be." He felt his throat expand with each utterance. Her face was pink. Her eyes were rimmed with the kind of exhaustion that Addison did not know how to show with his body, but he had felt it, fatigue as dark and deep as a cavern, endless tunnels of exhaustion, in those final years of the marriage.

Ruby's leaving had drawn him out of that cave. He'd followed her. He'd followed her voice, both irked and smooth, her words, black and white, and her smile, a flash of light in the opening. He'd trailed her decision to step into a new life with vibrancy and firmness. Her leaving helped him to feel more secure in his position, his life on the mountain. He did not want her crumpled on his kitchen floor. He wanted her glib and perky, spitting fire, romping, cavorting, revving up her bike and flying like lightning down the hill and away.

"I didn't know how to be with you," he repeated. The words came easily now. "Now I do. I do know how to be. How I like to be." He looked away and out the kitchen window at the pick Wren left perched on the outside sill. "You go back to Carl. You two suit each other." He patted her shoulder and kissed her on top of her head.

She folded her legs into a sitting position and leaned back, her shoulders spread, back arched, her hands on the floor supporting her. She smirked. "Well," she said. "The man has finally grown a pair."

She laughed. He didn't. He stood looking down at her. He noticed the cobalt blue lace peeping from the V of her shirt, and how her small breasts were propped by a thick padded bra; he could see that through her thin shirt. But the peak of her glaring cleavage did not warm him or stir him. For most, it might have, but like the women in his life had said, he was a strange guy. Instead, her liberation gave him a sense of peace. In actuality, this Ruby was the true Ruby.

"Becoming more of the person you always wanted to be is all anyone can ask," he said. It felt good to say that. "I'll meet you outside."

Addison put on a jacket and grabbed a bag of oilseed in the mudroom. He stepped outside. He now welcomed the sharp April air, how it was damp with promise, and how it cleared his head. He crossed the lawn around back to the bird feeders and slid the seed through a funnel into the tubes hanging in the leaf-bare hydrangea. After all the drama—

the pot, the tears, Ruby sprawled on the floor—filling the feeder, a tangible act, was a source of satisfaction and comfort for Addison. He planned to enjoy the mob of birds when he drank his coffee the next day.

At the kitchen window, he picked up the hoof pick. The iron felt warm from the sun. He peered into the house through the window. Ruby was gone. Had he been too harsh? He heard her start up her bike out front with an extra rev of the engine. She'd be just fine. She'd be happier now with Carl.

He walked around the house to see her off. As he watched her wind down the dirt driveway from the top of his mountain, it occurred to him, that if he was ever asked such a question again by a woman, a question not exactly like Ruby's wanting to drive home with another man, of course, but if he ever found himself in a similar situation, he would put the question back to her. He would ask the woman, *Who is it that you want to be?* It would sound odd, of course, out of context, perhaps, or untimely, very odd. But nonetheless, he would ask.

The Physics of Light

Sky can't sleep. Not because of his girlfriend, Emily, spooned next to him, the blanket sliding off her shoulder. She's beautiful, wicked smart, a good person. He knows he's lucky, but the image of Meredith Webb working alone in her studio is ghosting his thoughts.

He turns on the reading lamp over the bed. Emily mutters in her sleep. He tugs the blanket revealing more of her skin, creamy white and freckled. Her scent is lemon shampoo and sweat. He lifts his camera—his Canon F-1, a treasured hand-me-down—from the nightstand and snaps a picture. She can sleep through anything.

"Hold still," he whispers for his own benefit. Her auburn hair, a thick braid, ropes her back and snakes the sheet rumpled at her waist. He blurs the focus for a few more shots. "Perfect."

She wore her hair loose that day last September when he saw her in the financial aid office. Long curls floating down her back drew him, then the curve that met her hips. When she turned, saw him staring, she arched an eyebrow and smiled. She'd grown up here, played tag, went to middle school dances and ball games, but moved to Boston during high school. That day he first saw her again, she seemed brand new. She had come back from somewhere else.

That was nine months ago. Yesterday they took a break from cramming for finals and looking after her little sister. A rare Saturday, just the two of them. Emily posed for him in the woods behind her house on the flat granite ledge that flanks Stark Run—the river this town is named after—flooded with snow thaw, the sun streaming light through still branches. She removed an article of clothing, one at a time.

"Now arch," he said over sounds of rushing water. "Now curl."

She arched. She curled. That was for art, and then she pinned him and they screwed on last autumn's leaf debris speared with May fiddleheads all around. His camera never left his hands. Red maples blushed against the blue sky above. He snapped pictures of the shaggy red buds on the branches, the clouds overhead, and her.

He spent two rolls of film, a roll of black and white, and a roll of color, because spring was all about color after a gray and grainy winter.

Some of the stills he processed would never make it into his one-man show at the end of the week, this being too small of a town, and his mother parading her friends through the gallery in the student center, but he would always have those shots, memories of that day—for his eyes only.

Lying in bed wanting to lick Emily's shoulder, knowing she'd be pissed at him for waking her, he distracts himself by thinking about her twelve-year-old sister in the room down the hall. He understands how Emily needs to show up for Charlotte right now—their mother having checked herself into a treatment center—and according to her, if Sky is in this all the way, he shares the load. He's fond of Charlotte. She likes to spar, keeps him on his toes. But is he ready to go from being a kid to living with a girl who's in charge of a kid? He thought he and Emily would have more days like yesterday in the woods.

Emily shifts to her back. The sheet slides to her waist. Sitting now, he raises his camera, then thinks better. She snores. The air in the room is heavy. The gibbous moon casts a buttery light on the walls. He pulls the sheet to cover her, throws the quilt off his legs, and steals away.

Sky prowls the neighborhood, camera in hand. A row of bungalows crouch on River Road sandwiched between Main Street and the banks of Stark Run. Town Hall, Sweetbriar Inn, and the First Congregational Church cluster the only intersection with a traffic light. Shops line the street. The school where he rode the bus down the hill from the farm to attend kindergarten through the middle grades abuts the park. The high school, a converted paper mill, looms over the cemetery across the way. Streetlamps cast gloom on the town asleep. Picture perfect, he thinks. He can feel the his lips form a sneer.

He pulls a small tripod from his pack and snaps a few shots—mailbox, tourist information kiosk, and the closed sign in the window of the bakery—but he isn't out here for art, per se. He imagines his midnight roams are practice for some future adventure, Boston or New York. Maybe he'll check out Philadelphia.

Right now, he wants the stars. Growing up on a farm means that you can stand in the middle of a soggy hayfield at night and feel the Milky Way as if it touched your skin. In town, you only catch a marginal view. He walks to the park.

He sets up again and snaps three more shots—a new bench made of recycled plastic, a blue and bulky leather swing dangling from the old iron set, and a tree branch crawling the sky, all singular subjects, rendered grainy by the night. He walks backwards, shooting as he goes, careless about outcome, away from the playground area to the baseball diamond. He lies down, the back of his head on the mound where he pitched little league games. He sets his camera on his chest and imagines capturing random images of the universe, some stars, mostly moon, as if holding his breath to steady the lens during the exposure could capture the all of it, with impeccable clarity, exactly the way he sees it.

The ground dampens his flannel shirt, a chill seeps into his skin. He thinks about Emily, her body—always glowing, so warm—the blankets they share, a cocoon. He makes himself lie on the bare earth until he shivers. It's his ritual to grow cold of Emily, and then walk to Meredith's on the south end of town.

Meredith's house radiates in comparison to others on her street. Last August, he painted her clapboards marigold yellow, an odd choice among the more traditional homes, but standing here, seeing it in the moonlight, it makes sense to him that hers would outshine the rest.

Sometimes while he painted or trimmed shrubs, she talked to him, and he liked that more than the times she didn't. She had taught his art class senior year. She convinced him to go to community college until he was ready to go further afield, and then recommended his professor, Willis, an old-school photographer who still taught the dark room techniques that Sky loves. She understands him and he thinks Meredith's art is far too luminous for this old town. She doesn't belong here any more than he does.

From the driveway, he has a long view of the studio in the back corner of her yard. Like most nights, lamplight spills from the picture window into the shadows. He imagines her sitting on the stool at her draft table, the way he often saw her last summer, her hands poised over her work, still, her small frame lost in an oversized nightgown, white, or some other clothes that belonged to her dead mother. He got why she might want to wear her mother's clothes, but more, how a person can show one thing to people on the outside and live a different life altogether when they're alone.

Through the zoom lens of his camera, he focuses on the building, but is not close enough to see her. She can't see him, of course, because of distance and the physics of light. He considers walking back there, knocking on the door, but he doesn't want to disturb her. He knows she needs this time for her work.

He leans against the garage, craving a cigarette. Though he smoked very few times in his life, he wants to now. He likes the way people who smoke look, as if they harbor some secret trouble. A few months back, Willis told Sky to try and capture something remarkable about his subject, an essence that would make his audience feel uncomfortable. Now he seeks and finds discomfort in everyone, but particularly in Meredith, the way her eyes are often shadowed, her mouth turned down, her mind somewhere else.

He pulls up his collar to guard against the cool night air, wishing he'd worn his jacket, and paces the sidewalk, camera bumping his chest. He clenches his fists. He shivers. He should go home, climb in bed, and warm his body. He should at least be shooting film. It's what Willis tells him— keep working, never stop—and why Sky likes the camera: there's always something for his hands.

He stops and faces Meredith's house, which seems taller now in the pink light of dawn. He angles his shot to capture the slip of sky above the roof, just enough light now. He hears the creaky hinge on the studio door. He'd meant to oil it—it was on his list—all those months ago. He grips the camera tighter in his hands.

At the general store Sky buys a large coffee and a pack of cigarettes from Wren, who lifts her eyebrows. She's his mom's best friend, so she'll probably tell, but he's not sure he cares. Back at Emily's, he lurks in the driveway and lights up.

"When did you start that?" Charlotte asks. Emily's little sister sits on the back stoop chomping a bagel.

"Shit. You scared me." He throws the cigarette down and heels it with his boot. He throws the butt into the bushes. "What the hell are you doing up?"

"You wouldn't know, would you?" She stands and brushes crumbs from the rainbow tutu she wears over bright blue leggings and tightens the yellow laces of her bubblegum-pink sneakers. She looks lost in Emily's denim jacket. Part of him wants to snap a shot of her just like that, on the steps, hunched in the dawn light, and the other half wants to scoop her up in a brotherly hug, but he knows he can't do either. She's been through too much. It's made her prickly.

Charlotte tramps across the short yard past him. She digs his cigarette butt out of the bushes. She spits on it and drops it in the trash can on the curb.

"Sorry about that," Sky says.

"Only losers smoke."

He shoves his hands in his pockets. "Do you need a ride some place, Charlie?" If he makes the effort, Emily will purr over him all morning long, plus Charlie did seem a bit extra forlorn.

"Don't call me that." Her voice shouts across the sleepy Sunday neighborhood. She heads down the sidewalk towards town.

"Alrighty, then," Sky says and climbs the porch stairs into the house.

In the kitchen, Emily sits at the table reading her A and P textbook, biting the end of a highlighter. She wears Sky's best flannel, open, over his Twenty-One Pilots t-shirt. She sits in a crouch, bare legs folded, heels on the seat of the chair. Her arms wrap her knees. He imagines her body underneath the layers of his shirts. Her dismantled braid kinks and shrouds her shoulders. He raises his camera.

"Stop, Sky," she says, not looking up.

"What? Today you mind?"

"I'm just waking up," she says. "Where were you? You left your cell phone on the counter."

"I was out shooting landscapes."

"There's coffee and a bagel."

"Thanks." Normally he'd pull up a chair and try to make out with her until she shoved him off. He likes the taste of her coffee mouth. But the atmosphere of the room is chilly. "Everything okay with Charlie? She's up early." He leans against the refrigerator shining an apple on his jeans.

"She has the bakery job." She turns to him. "Remember?"

"Ah, right. Jeez." He rubs his face. "Guess I'm just waking up, too." He takes a bite of the apple.

"I have a study group this afternoon until late. I'm so fucking behind on my chapter notes."

"Got it. I'll spend the day in the darkroom. I'll just grab stuff and get out of your way." He gestures with the apple. "Want half?"

"Sure. Leave it on the counter." He hoped he could bring the apple over and feed it to her by mouth, bite by bite, his to hers, like they usually do. Instead, he takes a dessert plate from the drying rack, white with yellow daisies, sets the half-eaten fruit on the plate, and snaps a shot. In the open laundry room just off the kitchen he rummages through a bin on the shelves, looking for new film.

"Sky," she says. She purrs the y-vowel.

"Yep."

"Yesterday was good."

He turns and approaches her. She puts up her hand. "Nope."

They laugh and Sky wonders why he can't just be satisfied with her and this, the mixture of seduction with the focus on a practical future.

"I don't have time now," she says, and stretches her arms over her head as if to say she wishes she did have time.

"I get it." He puts his hands in his pocket. "Maybe we could talk after dinner. I want to show you the new stuff I got. I have to print and submit my twelve best by Wednesday. I need your eye. Plus you're in a bunch of them."

"Use your discretion on those. I trust you." She unfolds, stands, and forms her body into a tree pose. "Study group meets here until 10:00. Can you be back in time to make dinner for everyone so we can just push through? There are six of us and Charlotte needs help with decimals."

"Sure." As soon as he agrees, he wishes he said he was busy. He doesn't want to always be the stand-up guy.

"You're the best." Emily blows him a kiss. "I'm off to shower." She twists her braid and knots it with her highlighter.

He wants to run kisses along her neck, but he turns away to restock his camera bag. After, he pinches half of a burnt bagel from the old steel toaster on the kitchen counter. He eats it dry, hears water running and Emily singing. He thinks about her soaping her thighs. If he joined her, he could flush the deep-set chill from his body, but she's made herself clear. Instead, he thumbs a text message to her. *Will shop for burritos.* He finds the grocery money jar empty. He'll be dipping into his travel savings again. In the yard, he takes a piss in the weeds by the shed. He feels for the pack of cigarettes in his shirt pocket. Emily didn't notice them, or if she did, she didn't say anything. She'd be cool with it. Most girls wouldn't.

He lights up and walks behind the house and down the bank to take shots of the river ledge scene without Emily in it. He wants to do a series, tell a story, twelve images starting with Emily half-clothed on the rocks, then asleep in bed. He'd use the night shots from the empty park— zoom in, zoom out, blackness. If they were any good, they would punctuate the narrative. He'd place an image of the vacant riverbed at the end. The audience could interpret the linear progression however they wanted based on their personal view of the world—beauty, love, nature, loss. He won't push it too hard; he'll do what Willis said. Invite his audience to feel.

When Sky steps outside after a full day in the darkroom, his vision skews from being inside, and in his mind he keeps seeing his prints hanging in rows to dry, the final set for the show. When he reaches the end of the block he realizes how late it is. The phone in his pocket died hours ago. If he goes home, Emily will give him the look, and later, when her group leaves, she'll rant. By now they'll have ordered pizza. He can help Charlie later and figure out a way to make it up to Emily. He can't stand the idea of having a box of finished prints, ready to mount, and no one to run them by. He knows where to go.

Meredith's house is dark except for the flash of the television Sky can see through the sheers on her windows. It's too early for her studio vigil. He walks around to the backdoor and knocks, softly at first. When he hears no movement, he knocks louder. The kitchen lights flare and startle him.

"Sky!" She speaks through the screen door. "What's going on?"

She's wearing gray sweatpants and an over-sized baby blue t-shirt with an angel on it. Her hair is pulled back in a ponytail like a teenager.

"I'm sorry." He runs a hand through his hair. "I just finished work on a project. My pictures. I have this event at the college. They're due in three days. I need some advice and I thought of you."

She looks at her wristwatch.

"I know I should have called." He crosses his arms over his chest and rocks on the heels of his boots. "It was an impulse."

"All right, come in."

He sets his backpack on her kitchen table. In all the weeks he worked for her—weeding, painting, fixing the fence—he'd never stepped inside the house. It's the same layout as every other house in this part of the neighborhood, an old cape, except here, the kitchen cabinets have been remodeled and the clutter-free counters gleam with quarried stone. Art hangs everywhere, small art in small places. Scraps of wood carved into fish and birds and hand-thrown pottery deck open shelves above the stove. Sky walks around and marvels. Black and white photographs pepper the refrigerator, images of a child and a woman, mother-daughter portraits, he suspects, at all stages of life.

"Who took these?" he asks, turning to her.

"A friend of my mother's. He was my father figure." She makes quotation marks in the air and frowns.

"They're really good."

She nods. "That's why I leave them there." She sits down at the table. "Well that, and the obvious reason," she says.

"You miss your mom."

"Yeah, I miss her."

There's silence. He wonders if he should sit.

"So what did you bring?" she asks. "Show me."

Sky blushes. The excitement and pride he felt earlier, outside in the big air, now leaves him. He feels like an intruder. Sometimes he feels that way around Emily, too, when she and Charlie kick him out of the house for a girls' night in, or when Emily wants him to sleep somewhere else for a few nights so she can focus more on Charlie. He stares at the backpack on the table wondering if the body of work he brought to show her is too small in scope.

"Sky, relax."

He reaches into his satchel and pulls out the file folder box. "I want to place them in a series, the way they'll be in the show."

"Fine. I'll make tea. Use the floor. I mopped this afternoon."

He crouches and sets the prints out in order, creating a "u" of images.

"Are those cigarettes in your shirt pocket?" she asks.

He clutches the pack. "Shit. I forgot I had those. Sorry."

"Don't be sorry. I just didn't know you smoked. Here." She hands him a mug of tea. "Let me take a look."

"Well, they start here in the woods." He sweeps his free hand above the first trio of images.

"I can see that," she says, lifting an eyebrow.

He presses his palm to his chest to steady the pounding inside and takes a sip. Chamomile.

"She's a compelling subject," Meredith says. "The hair. Her skin."

"Right?" He holds the cup to his nose to smell the pineapple scent of the herbs. His mother used to grow chamomile and make tea from the flowers when he and his siblings got the stomach flu, which resembles the state he is in now, sweating, his gut roiling. He wills the herbs to soothe him.

"Sky, you're too nervous. Go stand over there."

She points to the door. Cool air sweeps through the screen, washes over him, and calms his jitters.

"I didn't think I'd be so nervous."

"Shhh."

The clock above the refrigerator is a vintage reproduction, fire engine red. It ticks off the seconds. It's almost ten, Charlie's bedtime, Sunday, laundry night, Sky's turn to fold. He thought he wanted this, to be in Meredith's house, to discuss art and the possibilities of art to make a statement, to show something to the world, and maybe get her to talk more about her time in Philadelphia when she was his age and all she had was paint and paper and the freedom to see inside herself and what else might be out there.

He steps onto the little porch. Clouds cover the moon and stars. He can't see a thing. He wants to run to the park and lie down in the field until he cools enough to walk back to Emily's and pull clothes, warm and clingy, from the dryer. He wants to deflect Emily's reprimands with flirting and fold her shirts and socks, fling a thong at her head while she studies at the kitchen table.

Meredith joins him on the porch. She carries a candle lantern, a bottle of Scotch, and two shot glasses on a small tray.

"Sit." She gestures to the wicker chair next to the loveseat. A blanket drapes her shoulders. She let her hair out of her stubby ponytail and wears a wool hat. She tosses a similar hat on the table next to the liquor bottle.

"Ninety-five percent of your body heat escapes out the top of your head. It's cold tonight. You should wear it." She sounds like his mother, but pours him a shot.

Sky ignores the hat and throws back the whiskey. Meredith takes a second shot and offers him another. After their third, she becomes still. She looks vulnerable all bundled up and curled into herself. He thinks about photographing her in this state. Emily, on the other hand, is strong and competent, shoulders back even when she studies. She takes over his lens. It's almost too much.

"So, what did you think?" he asks.

"Give me a cigarette."

"You smoke?"

"Rarely. Tonight I do. We drink. We smoke." She holds her pointer finger to her lips, a signal—our little secret.

He fumbles in the pack, finds two, lights them, and inhales hard. He hands one to her, leans back in his chair. The nicotine renders him sharp. He'll take whatever she has to say.

"It's nice to have company," she says. "But, Sky. I'm a teacher."

"Got it, but no one would mind, would they? The high schoolers wouldn't. They love you."

"Some would mind, many, actually. And I teach in the elementary school, too, don't forget." She blows a series of five smoke rings, each one growing smaller than the one before. "And this is Stark Run."

They laugh. They stare at the candle and smoke. He hasn't felt this good for months. Being out and about in the night, hanging with Meredith, whiskey in his veins, he feels like someone else, as if they aren't in a town where everyone knows everyone's business and you have to hide your smokes, as if a minute ago he wasn't longing for the kitchen at Emily's. Meredith flicks ashes off the side of the porch. Sky does the same.

"The photos are good, Sky, no doubt about it. You've got the light and dark thing down and your settings are smart. You're intuitive. You have an eye for composition, as they say." She sips. He hears her swallow. "They tell a story as stand-alones, most of them, and together, well, you've got a narrative in there, too."

"Thanks. That means a lot." He lets out a breath. He can tell she has more to say. "And . . ."

She laughs. "Look, you show up here late on a Sunday night, a school night, and catch me off guard. If I told you, *great show, now go home*, that would piss you off because, Sky, you've got pictures in there that show way more than the ones you've set out."

"You looked?"

"The point is, you know there's something more you have to do for this project, something difficult."

She leans forward and the blanket slips from her shoulders. The face of the angel on her shirt distorts and Meredith's eyes shine in the candlelight. She's otherworldly now and it conjures a mild fear in him. He shakes his head. She stubs her cigarette on a heart-shaped rock in a bowl set out for decoration.

He stands. "I'm supposed to know what that difficult thing is, aren't I?"

"You know."

"I do?"

"Yes."

He can't be sure. He's a little pissed that she looked through his private stuff and he's also a little pleased. He steps off the porch into the yard, tips his head back in search of a break in the clouds, a tiny disruption in condensation where one sparkle of star life can be witnessed from below by the one person interested enough to look, but the night is dark and the air thick with moisture. It smells like a time for new growth and toads. It feels like rain. The fields need it, and the salamanders, and the woods, too. He thinks it's funny how easily he slips back into thoughts of weather and critters, always the farmer.

Life on the farm is what he knows without a doubt, unlike the art stuff and the relationship stuff, just as he knows that even though it seems like rain, it is not going to rain, not tonight, not for a couple more days, and he wonders what Meredith did with her cigarette butt after she stubbed it out, and what he should do with his because Charlie would care. He rubs the butt on his jeans and puts the spent filter back into the pack in his pocket. It's chilly out here. He longs for Emily's bed. He climbs onto the porch.

"I guess I'll have to sleep on it, Ms. Webb."

"Meredith."

"Right."

"I'm sorry if I threw you," she says. "You seem thrown."

"I'll figure it out. I have a ton of other prints to consider."

"Okay, straight out advice time now, so listen up."

She pours another round. She drinks. He drinks.

"Follow," she says.

She gathers the bottle and their glasses. He trails her into the kitchen, finds his series of twelve photographs already picked up from the floor and placed on the box next to his backpack. He shakes his head.

"I'm not sorry I pried, Sky. You barged in here. Why waste time?" Meredith drops the blanket from her shoulders to a kitchen chair and turns to wash the glasses in the sink. "You need to consider all of the shots you have."

"I can't use those. She didn't say I couldn't, but I just couldn't."

"Well, let's say you can't use them. What about them, do you think, is what you need for this show?"

He closes his eyes. He feels tired from the lack of sleep and the whiskey. He sways. The blurred shots of Emily in bed, her vulnerability, and the expression on her face, lips parted during sex, they're intimate.

"The honesty," he says.

"Yes." Meredith spins around. "They're all about the *dream*, the *desire*." Her eyes flash.

"But I can't use those."

She dries her hands on a towel. "I get that. I do. But I've seen every one of them." She holds her hands together as if in prayer. "They're the really good ones. The honest ones."

The silence takes up space, but in a good way. As he considers the photos of Emily, he imagines that she's considering them, too.

"Have you tried cropping out just enough of her face?"

"I tried. Epic fail."

She pulls her lips in and nods. "Okay."

She slides the hat from her head, takes a brush from the kitchen drawer and fluffs out her hair. "Grab all your stuff and come with me."

Sky follows Meredith out the back door and across the lawn to her studio. A motion sensor throws on the light above the door, startling him, casting eerie shadows from the trellis onto the garden.

He's been inside her studio before and knows that she's guarded. He waits on the doorsill. From there, he watches her switch on the floor lamp by an old couch, red plush and worn, strewn with flowery mismatched pillows. She tips the lampshade to direct light onto the pile of cushions. She lights two candles on an end table. Unsure of what he should do, he fiddles with the toggle on his camera strap.

"Turn off the porch light and come in," she says. "Close the door."

It's nearing dawn when Sky walks in the direction of Emily's house. The cool air and the familiar shape of Main Street help to quiet the banging in his chest, which has simmered to a quick beat. He feels the way he felt as a boy when he woke up the first day of summer vacation. He remembers throwing off his blankets and leaping into what seemed a long stretch of time, fields and ponds and tree forts, pick-up baseball games when he could get a ride to town, freedom. He realizes how much he covets that sense of lightness.

He's grateful that the town is still. The only sign of human activity is the soft glow from inside the bakery. Sky imagines the doughy scent that will soon waft into the streets and linger for the rest of the morning, something he will miss about Stark Run, but right now he's noticing how the houses and trees, mailboxes, signs, and sleeping cars look more distinct, the contrast between light and shadow deepened, the shape of objects enhanced. He senses a narrative, too, not about the people and places that surrounded his childhood, but a broader scope: a prehistory, a present moment with his eye at the center of it, and a blank page. The expanse of that page lifts him.

Sky wakes to find Emily gone. When he crept in, she was already conked out on his side of the bed, the house dark and grim. Now his phone buzzes by his ear. There are three texts from his mother, one from his bio lab partner, and a notification from his calendar, *Office Hours-Willis*, but nothing from Emily.

In the kitchen he looks for a note. Charlie comes in from outside carrying the recycling container. Trash day. She's dressed in her gym uniform.

"You're in for it," she says almost singing.

He rubs his face. "Yep."

"It's about time you two figure out that it's just not meant to be."

"What are you talking about?"

"You guys have different goals."

"What do you know about it, Charlie?"

"Emily likes to help people."

"So do I." He can't believe he's arguing with a kid.

"I'm not so sure about that." She pours granola and milk into a bowl and sits down at the table. "She likes you, and she wants to see you figure stuff out, but she thought you'd be more mature."

"What the fuck?"

"That's a quarter." Charlie gestures to the swear-word jar they keep on the counter.

"Fine," he says. He reaches in his pocket, pulls out a dollar bill, and stuffs it into the jar. "It's all I have, so I'm good for three more." He turns a kitchen chair around and straddles it, the way he likes to sit when he wants to prop his head on his arms across the back. Charlie continues crunching her breakfast.

"God-damn it to hell, tell me what the fuck she said."

"Real mature, Sky." She opens her social studies book. "I'm studying. Besides, I'm too young for this. You'd better talk to her yourself."

Sky picks up a banana from the fruit bowl, but decides not to peel it. He's a little hung over. His concern for Emily casts a gloom on his memories of the night before. The clinking sound of Charlie's spoon pelts the silence. When she's finished eating, she sets her bowl on the floor for the cat to lick.

"Rinse it," he says.

"Fold the laundry," she replies. "It's your turn. You blew it and now all I have clean is this gym suit."

"Go to school." He rubs his temples.

"Gladly." On her way out, she slams the screen door.

Sky's phone buzzes: a text from Emily. *Super pissed. Plan for a long talk after finals. Let's get through the week.*

He looks around the cluttered kitchen. Dishes pile in the sink. Cupboards need painting. The refrigerator rattles, shaking the coupons hitched under magnets on the door. He picks up the F-1 and shoots rays of sunlight streaming in through a prism hanging in the window setting sparks of colored light onto the steel toaster, half of his burnt bagel from yesterday peeking up from the slot.

Over the next three days, with Emily and Charlie frosting him out of the house, Sky spends as much time as he can at his studio cubby on campus. He trawls through his portfolio from the year, chucking some of his prints, sorting piles——good, better, best. He takes breaks in the butt hut, not caring who sees him smoke, and imagines Meredith posing for him.

On Thursday, Willis approves Sky's series for the show—the prints he originally set out before Meredith—and gives him a B. Sky doesn't argue. The work is just okay. He shakes Willis's hand and walks out.

Friday evening, when it's time to leave for the show, Sky tells Emily and Charlie that he has a call to make and that he'll catch up with them at the student center. Emily cocks a brow as if she wants to say something, but they both agreed to hash everything out after all of their school stuff is over. She looks lovely in her cream sundress and light-blue cardigan with the tiny pearl buttons, her face and neck pink from sitting out in the yard in the spring sun, her cleavage teasing-white.

Charlie wears Christmas plaid PJ bottoms and a Captain America t-shirt. She cradles a grocery bag with snacks for the opening. "Whatever," Charlie says. She pulls her sister by the sleeve of her sweater. "Let's just go."

With the house empty, he collects his things, stuffing what he can into his backpack. He fills a box from the garage with film gear and a couple of books. He washes all the dirty dishes and sponges the kitchen counters. He writes a note and leaves it on the table.

> *Dear Em—*
> *I'm going for it. Heading to Philly. I feel like such a shit, but it's something I have to do. I'm sorry I'm not the guy you needed and I'm sorry about the show. I couldn't face the good-bye right now. I'm the first to admit I've got some things to work out. I'll call from Philly and hope to hell you pick up. Be well, Em.*
>
> *Yours, Sky*
>
> *PS Charlie, I know you're reading this. Take care of your big sis. You're the smartest kid I know.*

On the back stoop he lights a cigarette. Dragging nicotine into his lungs feels good, but when he thinks about it, smoking isn't him, and nothing, not smokes, not Scotch, exhilarates like capturing the image that says it all. He heels the butt and throws the rest of the pack into the trash can on the curb and then pulls the trash can to the side of the shed in the yard where Emily likes to keep it. He takes the woods trail along the river to the end of town and circles back to Meredith's.

At seven o'clock, it's still light out, getting lighter every day. Sky first knocks on the kitchen door and then crosses the yard. Meredith's studio sits empty. She said she'd be at the show and it looks as if she's keeping her promise. He drops his pack and lets himself in. He looks over at the couch area. The thrill of Sunday night sends a rush through his limbs. He smiles and shakes his head.

He sits on her stool and imagines it's still warm from her body. He rubs his palms on his jeans. A stack of sketches in ink lies on her draft table. She has penned the house, the gardens, and a cocky little bird sitting on the fence. There's a drawing of the back porch, the wicker furniture, her mother, sitting on the loveseat wearing a nightgown and sipping a glass of wine. Meredith has washed the pen and ink forms with watercolors—browns and grays, creams, and the bright yellow of the clapboards, even though the house had been white when her mother was alive. He likes how she took artistic liberties with reality. It says something. That she could see her mother sitting there now and that there's a fine line between, well, just about everything. He stacks her sketches. He pulls a note from his pocket. It's wrinkled now, greasy, and stinks of the half-eaten peanut butter protein bar he stuffed in there earlier. He smooths the note on the table alongside the sketches.

Meredith—I'm headed out tomorrow on the morning train. You were right, of course, I had to pull out the stops. It was the only way I could make a serious go of it.

Thank you. I'll text you my info. I hope
you'll continue to work. You're a born artist.
Ha! Listen to me. Thanks again for
everything.

He thinks the note lacks something. He picks up a charcoal pencil and adds: *Respectfully, Sky Ryan, your humble servant.* He sketches a rough image of the garden shed with a shovel leaning against it. He draws a cloud halfway covering a sun.

He rummages the tool bucket on a shelf in the garage, finds a can of WD-40 and oils the hinges of her studio door. He tests it. Perfect. He lifts his pack to his shoulders. On his way out, he passes through the trellis and grabs an errant creeper. He winds it around the main stem, tucking it out of the way. He walks in the middle of the quiet road to Main Street, directing himself, one foot in front of the other, to the student center.

At the art show, from the loft above where the computer station cubbies hide him from the crowd, Sky watches family and friends circulate through the displays. They hold small plates, cheese puffs, grapes, cashews, and plastic cups with soda water. Emily and Charlie have done a nice job with the snacks and he feels a thud of guilt in his gut.

Maeve Bellamy, his high school English teacher, is paired up with his Grandma Evaline. He wonders what Maeve thinks of the work, one of the people here who might actually get it. There's the dean of students and a handful of Sky's friends from his art classes. Most are clustered in groups around the work. His mother and father stand with Wren, Addison, and the Wileys at the food table.

"Who do you think it is?" Wren asks Molly.

Molly shakes her head. "Not Emily."

"He may have taken it a little too far," says Jack.

"Maybe, but good for Sky." Addison puts his arm around Wren's shoulder. "He's shaking it up a little. Good for the soul."

"Where the hell is he, Molly?" Jack asks.

"Not here. Not while we're all here. Right now I'm a little worried about Emily." They nod.

He sees Emily standing before one of the enlarged portraits. She gathers and ropes her loose hair over her right shoulder and is twisting the end. She's shaking her head, listening to Willis. Sky wishes he were the one explaining.

Charlie walks over to her. She's eating a cheese puff and looks up at Sky in the loft. She glares, and he expects her to call him out, but she turns away and pulls on Emily's hand. "Let's go."

Sky is struck by sadness deeper than he expected to feel as he watches his mom give Emily and Charlie a hug. Wren picks up empty cups and napkins. Jack is telling Addison and Willis some stupid story about a cow. People are trickling out.

Sky is about to leave when he sees Meredith walk in. The heavy gray feeling that waved in and settled in his chest at the sight of Emily walking away dissipates and he's energized, the way he felt in the darkroom all week, working alone, as if Meredith were there cheering his decisions. He now knows that when the eye behind the lens makes contact with the soul of the subject, everything the photographer views from that day forth carries an electric sheen.

He places his hands on the railing, leaning for a better view, no longer caring if anyone can see him. Meredith makes the rounds, chatting with a straggler or two, and studying the portraits. As she stands in front of the print where she's reclining on the couch, her face turned away, her hair not quite covering her breast, she pauses longer than she did before any of the other images.

It doesn't seem as if anyone left is making the connection to link her with the model in the work. He hopes Meredith is pleased with the outcome, his processing techniques, his rendering shadows to help conceal her identity when needed. He can't tell from her expression what she thinks, and since he won't be able to talk to her here anyway, he backs behind a cubby. Best not to tangle with Willis or his folks tonight. He'll hear from Meredith, sometime, in some way, when she's ready. He can wait.

At the park, Sky pulls a second sweatshirt over the first one. He lies down in the baseball field, sweaty from having wandered for miles. It's a cool night, though the continued drought has left the grass dry and he's certain he can sleep. He uses his pack for a pillow, places his camera on his chest. He keeps it here for comfort, no longer interested in taking pictures of this town.

He can't stop thinking about the heat Emily's body emits when she sleeps hard, one leg sprawled across his thighs, and how her hair falls like silk over his chest when she climbs on top in the morning.

The fact that his need to leave this town so far outweighs the comfort and satisfaction of her and all that they shared together makes him squirm. He shivers, curls to one side, his camera bulky against his chest. He puts his hands in a prayer position under his cheek.

At the train station, Sky sees right away that Meredith's little blue Civic is parked in the lot. He leans his backpack and portfolio against the car and lets himself in.

"I know you're not asking, but in case you're wondering, I do think leaving is best," Meredith says, the space between them shrinking as they sit parked in front of the platform. "You need to get away. See what else is out there."

"I feel like shit." He scrolls for texts and missed calls. "I pissed off more than a few people."

"True. So, now you need to get out of here and become a Stark Run legend."

They laugh.

"It doesn't have to be forever," she says.

He hears the sound of the train, the clanging, the rumble of the diesel. The smoky whistle makes him nervous, plants that small discomfort in his gut like the moment right before he has to pitch an inning.

"Can I call you later to talk about the show?"

"Absolutely."

He unfurls from the car. Meredith joins him on the platform. She's wearing the same over-sized clothes she wore the night they drank on her porch, her mother's clothes, out in the world for everyone to see.

"I admit it: I'm jealous." She looks up at him, shielding her eyes from the sun.

"You should be." Sky laughs. He gives Meredith a crooked hug, the bulk of his possessions pulling him off balance. He drops the portfolio against his knee, lowers his backpack, and pulls her in close. He knows the shape of her body well. Now he wants to remember how she feels, the strength in her smallness, and how she smells, the woozy scent of oils and turpentine, studio smells, mixed with whiskey and black tea. He inhales, taking it all in.

From his seat on the train, he watches her standing in the sun, arms at her sides, waiting for the train to pull out. He reaches for his camera, but then opts for his cell phone, adjusting the setting to the burst feature. He aims the lens at Meredith, the old brick station behind her, a peek of Main Street up the hill. This way, he can watch her with his bare eyes while recording the moment. Using his phone, he can keep the images close.

As the train pulls away, he touches the white dot on the screen. He's going for a ghost effect, Meredith among wisps of light, the specter-colors blurring most of the background.

A note from the author

Many years and a cadre of supporters went into the creation of this book. What began as a few stories written at Vermont College of Fine Arts grew into a fictional town and a community of imagined characters that became as real to me as the physical landscape and actual people who inspired me daily by their courageous lives. To that landscape and those great big Vermont hearts, I am eternally devoted.

I've been favored with the acute observation, literary aesthetic, and nurturing spirits found in my mentors and close readers: Trinie Dalton, Dave Jauss, Philip Graham, Mary Stein, Ross McMeekin, and Cynthia Newberry Martin. To program director Louise Crowley, and the students, faculty, and staff at Vermont College of Fine Arts, many thanks for your lectures, workshops, and chats, for your passion and commitment.

This project owes a great deal to the readers, editors, and guest editors of literary journals, those humble machines who championed a number of these stories early on: Vivian Dorsel, Robin Black, Matthew Limpede, Bridget Boland, Pam Houston, Brian Schott, Jacob White, Karen Stefano, and Ken Robidoux. Many thanks to Lori Ostlund for her sharp eye in the final round.

Without the vision of Kevin Morgan Watson, editor and publisher, this book would still be a digital file on my desktop. I am grateful for his laidback flow and attentiveness, equally measured as needed, and particularly for his guiding hand in "The Physics of Light." Press 53, an enthusiastic family of writers, readers, and artists, has been built with great care, one beautiful book at a time.

Thanks to Joe and Pat Paloni for encouraging my education, beginning at Upland Country Day School where the love of language and literature grew like fire. By some mysterious intervention, I was sent two extraordinary daughters and a benevolent spouse. Lizz, Luci, and Bob, your faith in me has been the oxygen.

To Suzanne Kingsbury, book shaman extraordinaire, who sprinkles magical word dust on everyone she touches, thanks for building the Gateless Writers Community and welcoming me with open arms.

Finally, to all of you readers, thank you, your devotion fuels the craft.

JODI PALONI's stories appear in a number of literary journals including *upstreet*, *Carve Magazine*, *Whitefish Review*, *Green Mountains Review*, *Connotation Press*, and others. Her work has won the Short Story America Prize and placed second in the Raymond Carver Short Story Contest. She holds an MFA from Vermont College of Fine Arts. Raised in rural Pennsylvania, she lived in Vermont for twenty-five years, and recently settled on the coast of Maine. *They Could Live with Themselves* was a runner-up for the 2015 Press 53 Award for Short Fiction and is her debut story collection.

Cover artist DAWN D. SURRATT studied art at the University of North Carolina at Greensboro as a recipient of the Spencer Love Scholarship in Fine Art. She has exhibited her work throughout the Southeast and currently works as a freelance designer and artist. Her work has been published internationally in magazines, on book covers, and in print media. She lives on the beautiful Kerr Lake in northern North Carolina with her husband, one demanding cat, and a crazy Pembroke Welsh Corgi.

CPSIA information can be obtained at www.ICGtesting.com
Printed in the USA
BVOW08s1928070316

439420BV00001B/18/P